"I'm sorry." She breathed against the middle button of his shirt. "I never fall apart like this. "

"You just need to get some sleep," he murmured gently. He rubbed soothing circles across her back, trying to ignore her sweet, inviting curves. His attraction to her was completely wrong, and yet, holding her like this felt completely right.

Her fingertips stroked his spine, as if trying to placate him. But at her gentle touch, a deep, illicit longing surged inside him. Man, he wanted to kiss her. He wanted to do other things, too. But he'd be content if he could just keep her in his arms throughout the night. If he could touch her and know she was safe, know she was with him.

"If you tell anyone that Shauna Cartwright is..."

What? Beautiful? Tough? Sexy? "Human?"

Her nod was a caress against his chest. "I'll put a reprimand in your file if you let that one slip."

Eli grinned. "Your secret's safe with me, boss lady."

JULIE MILLER

BABY JANE DOE

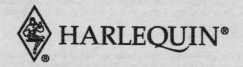

HARLEQUIN®

TORONTO • NEW YORK • LONDON
AMSTERDAM • PARIS • SYDNEY • HAMBURG
STOCKHOLM • ATHENS • TOKYO • MILAN • MADRID
PRAGUE • WARSAW • BUDAPEST • AUCKLAND

For Precious Doe (aka Erica Michelle Marie Green), whose tragic story inspired a police force and an entire city. And for the good, kind citizens of Kansas City, Missouri, who loved a little girl enough to create a lasting memorial to a precious angel.

While inspired by a real event, the details and characters of this story are entirely the results of the author's imagination.

ISBN-13: 978-0-373-88721-7
ISBN-10:   0-373-88721-3

BABY JANE DOE

Copyright © 2006 by Julie Miller

www.eHarlequin.com

Printed in U.S.A.

ABOUT THE AUTHOR

Julie Miller attributes her passion for writing romance to all those fairy tales she read growing up and shyness. Encouragement from her family to write down all those feelings she couldn't express became a love for the written word. She gets continued support from her fellow members of the Prairieland Romance Writers, where she serves as the resident "grammar goddess." This award-winning author and teacher has published several paranormal romances. Inspired by the likes of Agatha Christie and Encyclopedia Brown, Ms. Miller believes the only thing better than a good mystery is a good romance.

Born and raised in Missouri, she now lives in Nebraska with her husband, son and smiling guard dog, Maxie. Write to Julie at P.O. Box 5162, Grand Island, NE 68802-5162.

Books by Julie Miller

HARLEQUIN INTRIGUE

588—ONE GOOD MAN
619—SUDDEN ENGAGEMENT†
642—SECRET AGENT HEIRESS
651—IN THE BLINK OF AN EYE†
666—THE DUKE'S
    COVERT MISSION
699—THE ROOKIE†
719—KANSAS CITY'S BRAVEST†
748—UNSANCTIONED MEMORIES†
779—LAST MAN STANDING†
819—PARTNER-PROTECTOR*
841—POLICE BUSINESS*

880—FORBIDDEN CAPTOR
898—SEARCH AND SEIZURE*
947—BABY JANE DOE*

† The Taylor Clan
* The Precinct

CAST OF CHARACTERS

Shauna Cartwright—KCPD's most public face. The acting commissioner has her hands full with an unsolved murder, an anxious city and a possible saboteur on the force.

Eli Masterson—Kansas City's most private cop. An Internal Affairs detective still living down the sullied reputation of his corrupt partner. After saving his boss's life, a forbidden attraction develops.

Seth Cartwright—Shauna's son, a vice cop at KCPD.

Sarah Cartwright—Shauna's daughter. Unlike her overprotective twin brother, she likes the new man in her mom's life.

Austin Cartwright—Shauna's ex just won't stay away.

Michael Garner—Shauna's right hand in the commissioner's office.

Rebecca Page—Crime beat reporter. Just who is her inside source?

Yours Truly—Is his vendetta against the commish personal or professional?

Baby Jane Doe—Her unsolved case united an entire police force. But new evidence at her suspected killer's trial can rip the city apart.

Chapter One

Nice.

Three customers ahead of him, one window over in the lobby of the Cattlemen's Bank in the heart of downtown Kansas City.

Detective Eli Masterson didn't need the eye for detail he possessed to notice an attractive woman when he saw one. Her mocha-colored suit, a few shades darker than her short blond hair, hugged some prime feminine curves. The light wool skirt stopped just short of hiding the dimple at the back of her right knee. The sensible brown pumps that matched her leather shoulder bag didn't detract from the long arch of her calves. Even in heels, Ms. Tailored Professional Lady barely topped Eli's shoulder, putting her at average height. But he'd bet a good part of her was legs.

Long, fit, curvy legs, capped by that sweet butt. *Very nice.*

Eli breathed deeply, savoring the quickening rhythm of his pulse. A good, lustful look was about all he had time for these days. So he waited patiently and enjoyed his wayward private thoughts before he had to move to the front of the line and deal with reality again.

He'd taken the morning off because he had Jillian's hearing at ten o'clock. Today he was transferring what was left of his parents' insurance money into his checking account. His baby sister might be fined for possession, or more likely, she'd be sent straight to rehab again. Eli intended to be able to sign on the dotted line and drive her there himself. Maybe this time they could get her off her cocaine habit and make it stick. Lord knew he'd run out of ideas about how to keep her safe from herself.

He moved forward in line as the skinny kid at the front thanked the teller and turned. Despite the sunglasses and hooded sweatshirt, a passing glance revealed that the man at the front of the line wasn't a kid so much as a thirty-something who needed to lose the saggy pants and accept that gangsta was a look few people over sixteen could pull off without drawing undue attention to themselves. Of course, that was probably the point.

Eli's gaze slid back to the blond chick.

He'd much rather pay attention to her more subtle charms.

She didn't seem to mind the early-morning crush of customers, hurrying in to take care of business before they had to report to work themselves. She stood out from the others in line the way a froth of cream cooled his morning coffee.

He liked a woman who was calm and sophisticated, and buttoned up tight like her conservative suit. Women like that played relationships the way they conducted business. There were always rules to follow, barriers to respect. A man couldn't get in too deep with her, which suited him fine.

Intelligent conversation was good. Shared interests even better. Mutual lust was a bonus. But Eli knew enough about getting burned by emotional connections that once he detected any hints of personal commitment going on beneath the suit of a pin-striped pinup, he walked away from them as fast as his size thirteens could carry him.

Hmm. Not just a nice bod. She was observant, too. Blondie had noticed the over-the-hill rapper wannabe as well. She hesitated as she approached the teller window and turned her head ever so slightly to watch his departure.

Eli caught a glimpse of her profile and a spark of recognition tried to catch hold inside him. But she smiled and turned away at the teller's greeting before a name could click into place.

What *did* register was that she was older than he'd suspected from the rear view. But she wore it well. The fringe of hair that framed her face had blended into the clean contours of her jaw and cheek. And the hints beside her eye and mouth that she might be closer to fifty than forty hadn't appeared until they'd crinkled into view with her smile. Pretty as she was, Blondie probably had a successful husband, two-point-three kids and a house in the suburbs to go home to.

Ah, yes. Reality. Though certainly not his.

Time to tone his interest down a notch.

Another teller reported for early-morning duty at a third window, and Eli used the shifting of the waiting patrons to adjust his silk tie and find something new to study. The man with the gangsta look slipped into the elevator instead of exiting through the brass-trimmed glass doors. Maybe there was a problem with his account, and he'd been told to take it to one of the offices upstairs.

Eli rolled his neck against his crisp white collar. That scenario didn't sit right. The guy had been too friendly with the teller. A man with a problem would have raised a stink.

A second man, who stood out from the suit-and-tie crowd as much as over-the-hill gangsta had, swooped into Eli's peripheral vision at the new window. The tension in Eli's neck crept out across his shoulders. This guy wore a regulation business suit like almost everyone else, but he'd topped it with a long black trench coat. The calendar might say autumn, but it was still early enough in the season that the air hadn't crisped yet. There was certainly no chill to chase away on a sunny morning like this one.

Trench coat man wore a pair of mirrored Ray•Bans that he left on as he struck up a flirty conversation with the young woman who was still setting up her cash drawer. An internal sensor, borne of fourteen years on the force and a lifetime of cleaning up other people's messes, blitzed across Eli's nerve endings, warning him that something was wrong with this picture. Two men in sunglasses early in the morning? Eli shook his fists loose down at his sides and squeezed his left arm against the Glock holstered inside his jacket.

He slid his gaze back to the front door to the uniformed guard who had checked his badge and cleared his gun before allowing him to enter the bank. The young black man was focused on something out on the front sidewalk rather than on the *six, seven*—Eli silently counted them off—make that *ten* customers and staff here on the first floor. A second guard, as close to retirement as the other was to his rookie year, strolled through the lobby, chatting with customers and staff.

Blondie was curiously assessing her surroundings, too. Her movements slowed as she stuffed a bankbook into her purse and angled her head toward Mr. Trench Coat, watching him stride across the geometric designs of the carpet and disappear into the public restroom.

Eli was more suspicious than most cops. And those suspicions were eating at him now, making him fidgety inside his skin, though he allowed no trace of his thoughts to show. His instincts were to follow Mr. Trench Coat and verify that he knew something about the weather forecast that the rest of them did not. Though he prayed the man's unusual appearance had such a benign explanation, Eli's suspicions warned him otherwise. He tried to catch the guard's eye again to find out if the younger man had taken note of the two out-of-place customers.

"Good morning, sir. May I help you?" The teller's bright blue eyes smiled a greeting as she drew Eli's attention back to the teller's station. But Eli zeroed in on the three-piece-suited man behind her who shuffled out from the vault area with an expanding folder tucked under his arm. He stuffed his hand into his pocket, pulled out a white handkerchief and mopped at the perspiration dotting the top of his balding head. Then he nearly jumped out of his oxfords when the older guard greeted him from across the room.

Baldy managed a nod and a vague response. But the guy was sweating. In the air conditioning. The pasty skin from forehead to pate indicated the man was either having a heart attack or...

Damn. Eli's growing tension clenched through every muscle, then dissipated, leaving an icy chill of certainty in its wake.

Do *not* rob this place this morning.

He had to get to court. He had to be there for Jillian.

He didn't have time to be right about this.

Eli jerked his head from side to side. Elevator to the north. Bathroom to the south. Baldy behind the counter. A perfect triangle surrounding the customers, the guards and the money inside the tellers' drawers.

Glancing over his shoulder, Eli tried to catch the guard's eye at the front door.

Damn. Damn. Damn.

"Sir?" The teller's voice demanded action.

Eli leaned across the counter, pulling open the front of his jacket to flash his badge and whisper into the startled girl's ear. "Hit your silent alarm. Now."

"What?"

"Do it."

He didn't want to start a panic if he was wrong, but his gut told him he was right. Something was going down.

Blondie sensed it, too. She'd pulled her cell phone from her purse and was walking straight toward the older security guard. She touched the man's arm, urging him to mask his stunned expression. Blondie turned and faced Eli full-on, but she was pointing past him toward the public john.

What the hell?

Eli wasn't the only cop in the building.

Recognition did him little good now. There was no time to identify himself. No time to do more than to warn the teller to get off her stool and seek shelter down behind the counter. "Hit the ground. Now!"

The bathroom door swung open. The elevator dinged. Guns came out of billowing coats and saggy jeans. A thunderclap exploded outside and a blast of shattered glass and flying metal rained down inside the lobby. The young guard went down. A deadly staccato of semiautomatic gunfire erupted over their heads.

The older guard's hand never reached his gun. With a startled gape, he grabbed his chest and sank to the floor, taking Blondie with him. Eli glimpsed the red blooming beneath her hands as she crouched over the fallen guard and tried to staunch his wound.

"Take cover!" Eli shouted over the screams and chaos, grabbing the startled black man beside him and shoving him to the carpet. Others ducked behind the counter. In one fluid movement, Eli dove and rolled toward Blondie. He rose up on his knees, slung his arm around her shoulders and dragged her to the floor, tucking her beneath his long body as bits of ceiling and light fixtures and bullets crashed down around them. "Eli Masterson." He ground the words against her ear. "Detective. KCPD."

"GET OFF ME!" Shauna Cartwright ordered between tightly clenched teeth. She didn't know which angered her more—the senseless violence that left a man bleeding to death just beyond her reach, or the tall, muscular detective who'd wrapped himself so thoroughly around her that she could feel his holster jammed against her shoulder blade and smell his love for coffee on his breath.

His broad shoulders masked her view of the scene and absorbed the brunt of the debris raining down on top of them. Masterson had gone all macho to protect the perceived "little woman" while innocent bystanders cowered unguarded beneath the hail of intimidation shots. As though she couldn't take care of herself!

She'd spotted the body armor beneath the trench coat of the man who'd disappeared into the john. *She'd* alerted the guard, paged 911 and kept her head low when the bullets started flying.

Shauna squirmed beneath the immovable weight of the determined detective and repeated the command. "Get. Off."

But she went still beneath his surrounding warmth when the bullets abruptly stopped. She recognized the sound of the thieves switching out their ammo. Would they fire again? Choose more living targets this time? Could she reach her gun in her purse? Where *was* her purse? Was there any way to get to the two wounded guards and help them? The eerie silence after the deafening barrage of gunfire made her thoughts seem loud inside her head.

"Shh."

At the whisper against her ear, Shauna caught her breath, thinking for one crazy moment that she'd uttered her thoughts out loud and given herself away. She might have trembled as fear found a chink in the adrenaline charging through her system. And Detective Masterson's arm might have tightened imperceptibly around her, offering reassurance as well as protection.

For one deep, controlled breath, Shauna allowed herself to accept Eli Masterson's comfort. A man's personalized warmth and strength were a rare treat in her life, and for that one breath, she let herself be a woman who was sheltered and cared for.

But that wasn't who she was. With the next inhale, she became a cop again. And not just any cop.

An acrid cloud of gunpowder, plaster dust and fear stung her nose. But the only thing she reacted to was the shift of hard muscles against her back and bottom.

The instant she felt Masterson move, Shauna snatched at his arm, silently warning him to stay put. The detective could play cowboy on his own time. But not when there were hostages present. Not when the perps' intent remained unclear.

"Easy," she breathed against the dusty wool of his sleeve. Though he stopped moving, the tension in his body never relaxed. "Assess the situation before we act."

"Everybody stay put and no one else gets hurt!" The man in the trench coat took charge. The movement of his voice indicated that he'd gone behind the counter. "Get the documents and whatever cash you can grab."

Documents? Shauna frowned. So this wasn't a straight-out robbery. She should have guessed as much from an assault that had started with a precisely timed explosion.

As the voices moved farther away, the detective began a succinct report in her ear. "The situation is you've got two armed men, possibly three—"

"—the sweaty banker behind the counter?"

"Sharp eye." So Masterson had been suspicious of a possible setup, too. "Those guns were stashed so they could get past the guard. And who knows what's waiting outside? That could have been an unmanned bomb, a projectile shot—"

"These guys will have a getaway car waiting. This robbery's too well planned not to."

Masterson nodded agreement. "Early-morning strike. Minimal hostage risk."

Shauna wriggled a few inches of freedom from beneath him. "Those hostages should be our first concern. I need to get out and help the guard."

She had both arms free and was pushing up before the detective cinched his arm around her waist and pulled her back into the heated curve of his body. "Look who they took out first. I don't think these men would be too impressed to find out we're cops."

Turning her cheek into the carpet, Shauna looked into Eli Masterson's cool brown eyes. "You know who I am?"

"Yes, ma'am."

She supposed that was the curse of having such a public face. Detective Masterson thought he was earning brownie points. Fat chance. On a more charitable note, maybe he was just being a team player. If that was the case, she wasn't cutting him any slack. He should be obeying the chain of command.

Shauna pried his arm from her waist. "Then chances are, they do, too. Keep your sidearm holstered and don't try to be a hero." She got her knees beneath her and wrenched free before Masterson could nab her again. "I'm a trained negotiator. I've dealt with situations exactly like this one. I've already paged—"

"Backup's already on the way," he informed her. His hard exhale matched her own. "Stay put. Let these guys take what they want and walk out of here. They won't get far."

"You two. Shut up." The antsy thirtysomething, whose street-tough look lacked the bulk of his partner's Kevlar vest, leveled his Smith & Wesson at Shauna's forehead, silencing the debate. "Get behind the counter with the others."

But Shauna was insistent. She looked up along the gun barrel to his nervous, darting eyes. "That guard needs medical assistance before he bleeds out. I have first-aid training. You don't want this to turn into a murder scene. Let me help."

Without waiting for an answer, Shauna slowly rose to her feet, keeping her eyes on his the entire time.

"Okay. Hey! Not you, big guy." Shauna froze as he swung his gun toward Masterson, who deliberately ignored the order and stood up beside her. "Don't move!"

Though he held his hands up in surrender, Masterson towered a good four or five inches over the armed man, and the cold mask of his expression didn't so much as blink at the gun pointed his way. "I can help the other guard," he offered.

The man with the gun contradicted his own order and jabbed the gun into Masterson's chest, knocking him back a step. "Get behind the counter."

"Get him back here. Now!" The man in the trench coat appeared to be in charge of the robbery. He left the banker to cram what stacks of bills would fit into a briefcase already stuffed with files. He pointed his snub-nosed rifle at them as he whirled around the corner. "Do what we say and live. Okay, lady—help the cop." He shoved aside the other thief to personally back Masterson behind the counter. "You? Move!"

Though he'd mistakenly referred to the fallen guard as a member of KCPD, Shauna wasn't about to correct him. She hurried over to the wounded man, peeled off her jacket and pressed it against the hole in his chest, murmuring soothing words when he groaned in pain.

The guard's gun was still in his holster, within arm's reach—unlike her own weapon, which was ten feet away inside her purse. Of course, she shouldn't try to play hero, either. Not with hostages involved. Not when they were up against a semiautomatic rifle and a handgun with a fresh clip of fifteen bullets. And if they robbed the patrons, went through pockets and purses and discovered badges and guns...

She prayed KCPD's response time was as good as she'd claimed it to be in her last television interview.

"Is he gonna be okay?"

Shauna started at the perp's voice beside her. But the sniff of gunpowder residue clinging to him and his gun kept her from feeling any compassion at his remorseful tone. She didn't mince words. "He needs an ambulance." She tipped her head to the side, indicating the guard lying by the shattered front door. "I need to check him, too."

"He's moanin'. Breathin' normal. So he can't be hurt that bad."

"Internal injuries are hard to evaluate just by looking at a man." She let the shooter see her bloody hand before she wiped it on her skirt and smoothed the guard's white hair off his forehead. "Please let me call the paramedics."

"No can do." She could smell the sweat, fueled by fear, on him. "We're almost done. We'll be out in a minute and then you can call whoever the hell you want." He turned and shouted over his shoulder. "You got all the papers the boss wanted?"

"Shut up, bozo!" the man in the trench coat yelled. "Why don't you give them our names, too, while you're at it?"

Shauna could make out Detective Masterson's feet sticking out from the end of the counter. He'd cooperated by obeying the command to lie facedown on the floor. Thank God he wasn't stirring up any more trouble. She also caught a glimpse of movement outside. A uniformed officer moving some curious on-lookers who'd gathered across the street. She hoped his silent arrival had escaped the thieves' notice. And that he wasn't alone.

The man in the trench coat stepped over Masterson's prone body and leveled the gun at the banker who closed and locked the briefcase. "Is that everything?"

"Just like we…discussed." He stuttered when he got an eyeful of the gun barrel. "What are you doing?"

"Following orders." He pulled the trigger.

The banker slumped. Hostages shrieked in panic and cursed.

"Hell, man, are you crazy?" The man with the gun next to Shauna didn't seem to know where to point his gun now. "You said we were just gonna scare the crap out of 'em and nobody would get hurt."

"I lied." The other man turned his rifle and fired.

Shauna ducked as the shot hit the man square in the chest and knocked him off his feet. She didn't bother checking to see if she could help him. She knew a dead man when she saw one.

And she knew she was next.

Though she was already moving, the sinking

certainty slowed her reaction time. When Shauna lifted her head to locate the dead man's weapon, she looked up into the glint of fluorescent light reflecting off the shooter's sunglasses. She didn't need to see the eyes behind the lenses. They were focused on her.

Just like his gun.

Nanoseconds ticked off like eons.

He smiled.

Shauna dove for the floor.

He squeezed the trigger.

A gust of steel-tipped wind rushed past her ear. But the bullet never hit her.

"KCPD!" With the clean precision of a surgical blade, Eli Masterson put a bullet center-mass in the shooter's chest, knocking him off balance. The shooter stumbled backward but didn't fall. "Drop your weapon!"

But the man ignored the order and swung his gun toward the unexpected attack.

"Cease fire!" Staying low to the floor, Shauna picked up her cell phone and threw herself against the counter, keeping her back to the only protection the lobby offered her. "Dammit, Masterson, we've got hostages. Cease fire!"

"Negative!"

She redialed her 911 call and snagged her purse to retrieve her service weapon. From the low angle of the fire, Detective Masterson was down. Was he hit or had he taken cover?

"Masterson? Report!"

Shauna crawled to the end of the counter for a visual. The gunman lunged toward the elevator doors, chased by a hail of bullets, unable to return fire. Two more rounds hit the back of his trench coat. The man jerked, but stayed on his feet. The elevator doors opened. He jumped inside. Swung around. Raised his gun and grinned in triumph. "You're out of ammo."

Idiot!

She could kick herself for forgetting. "He's wearing a Kevlar!"

Before she could get her own gun aimed, Masterson rolled. As the doors drifted shut, he snatched up the dead thief's discarded Smith & Wesson and put a bullet in the killer's knee, taking him down.

The man in the elevator screamed in agony as Shauna and Masterson scrambled to their feet and approached, guns drawn.

"KCPD," Shauna announced in a clear, firm voice. "Drop your weapon and come out."

"Like I could, you bitch." Several more obscenities tainted the air, condemning KCPD and her own parentage, as well as promised retribution against the man who'd crippled him.

"Shut up." Detective Masterson's big brown shoe blocked the doors before they could close. With his gun trained on the wounded man, he pushed the doors open and picked up the rifle. He handed it to Shauna before stepping inside to lock the doors open and drag the man out into the lobby. "The lady said to move."

With the man's curses abruptly silenced by something whispered in his ear, Detective Masterson pinned him to the floor, patted him down for other weapons and cuffed him. "He's got no ID on him." He tossed aside the sunglasses and jerked the perp's chin up toward Shauna. "You recognize him?"

Icy gray eyes like that she would remember. "No. But we'll run his prints if he doesn't cooperate."

"Like I'm gonna—"

Masterson ground the man's face into the carpet, silencing him.

By the time the detective was on his feet again and holstering his gun, Shauna had retrieved the briefcase and given the dispatcher instructions for police and paramedics to move in.

Maintaining his protective stance over the perp, Detective Masterson glanced down over the jut of his shoulder at her. "You all right?"

Other than some bruises and rug burns she

wouldn't complain about, Shauna was in one piece. She nodded. "You?"

"He had you in his sights."

Shauna pretended his deep-pitched admonition didn't send an ominous chill through her veins. "I'm *fine*."

She took note of the two-inch cut oozing blood along the edge of his short, coffee-colored hair. But, for the moment, she ignored his forehead and watched the piercing intensity of his dark eyes cool to golden brown detachment. More than his 20/20 aim with the gun, they hadn't missed a detail of all that had transpired here. Not even the personal threat to her life.

Which Shauna refused to comment on. It was all part of the job, right?

She tucked her phone and the gun in the waistband of her tweed skirt and stuck out her hand for an official introduction. "I'm Shauna Cartwright."

"I know."

She waited until he took her hand. His grip was as strong and firm as the rest of him had proved to be. And though an often-ignored part of her wished she was meeting such a seasoned, attractive man under different circumstances, she knew succumbing to her feminine longings was out of the question.

"Eli, was it?" He nodded. "May I see your badge, Detective?"

A scoffing sound marred his smile as he let her hand go to reach inside his jacket. "I heard you were a tough one for rules and regs. Are this morning's events going into my file?"

Shauna ignored the taunt and quickly read the ID beside his badge. Eli Masterson. Thirty-six years old. Fourteen years on the force, the majority of them having filled a necessary but difficult role.

"Internal Affairs?" She glanced down at the man moaning at their feet. "And you made that shot?" She indicated the small gold star on his ID before handing it back. "Why would an I.A. detective maintain his sharpshooter's badge? You planning to transfer to S.W.A.T.?"

"No, ma'am."

"Does Captain Chang," she referred to the chief of the I.A. division, "have this much trouble getting you to cooperate with your fellow officers?"

"Yes, ma'am, he does."

She almost laughed at his dry delivery of the truth, and though she appreciated a man with a smart wit, she never allowed the humor to soften the taut curve of her own lips. "Well..., thank you for saving my life, Eli. You saved all our lives today."

He seemed hesitant to accept her praise. "No problem."

Leaning in, she caught him off guard as she nabbed his handkerchief from the pocket where he'd stuffed his wallet. She surprised him further by pressing the cotton to the wound on his forehead. "Make sure one of the medics clears you before you leave. I can't tell if that's a shrapnel cut or a bullet graze, but it looks like you could use a stitch or two."

It felt almost intimate, like a woman caring for her man, to stand there in the midst of the bustling recovery team, gently tending Eli's wound. She felt herself warming beneath the scrutiny of his gaze as he tried to figure out whether her kindness was genuine or a ploy he should guard against. His fingers brushed against hers as he took over staunching the wound and retreated a step. "I'll do that, ma'am."

"Good." Wouldn't it be nice to skip the *ma'am*'s for once and just be a woman with a man? But she was more than that. And the suspicion in Eli Masterson's eyes said he knew it, too. So she pulled rank. The way he expected. The way she was supposed to. "You got away with playing cowboy today, Masterson. But when I tell you to do something, I expect it to happen. The chain of command needs to be followed, no matter what the situation is."

"I'll remember that next time."

"Please do."

"Is that all?"

"I'll expect a report from you tomorrow."

"Yes, ma'am."

Shauna watched him turn and disappear into the crowd of officers, medics, CSI techs and curious thrill-seekers bustling about outside.

"Damn," she muttered, spotting the deputy commissioner, Michael Garner, breaking through the same crowd and flashing his ID to the scene commander. If the main office already knew she'd been involved in a shoot-out, that meant the reporters would be following shortly. Once the press got wind of this, her children would find out. They'd worry. But Seth and Sarah were adults now. She could handle them.

What worried her was the possibility that *he* would find out. *He* seemed to know every secret about her life. Shauna shivered with a chill that had nothing to do with the temperature of the air or the scene around her.

When Michael waved to her and hurried over with concern shining in his eyes, she wished she could disappear as easily as Eli Masterson had.

Michael certainly was an efficient one. He'd wasted no time in getting here. She glanced down at her bloody hands and the stains on her cuffs and skirt. Her appearance should earn a few personal questions she was in no mood to answer. If she asked, Michael would organize the reports from this deadly fiasco and handle the press. She could go home and clean up, lock her doors and isolate herself from the death and destruction surrounding her.

But she couldn't ask.

KCPD's Commissioner of Police didn't have that luxury.

Chapter Two

"Masterson."

Eli topped off the coffee in his plastic cup before acknowledging the unmistakable sound of authority behind him. "Captain Taylor."

"What brings you to my precinct?"

Though he doubted running into each other in the break room was a coincidence, Eli took his time before stepping aside for the patriarch of the Fourth Precinct to fill a Kansas City Chiefs mug with the thick, steaming brew. "Routine follow-up on the shooting by your man, Banning."

No sense wasting pleasantries. There was no love lost between Internal Affairs and the Taylors since Eli and his former partner, Joe Niederhaus, had investigated the captain's cousin, CSI Mac Taylor, four years ago. Especially since his old buddy Joe had done such a bang-up job of framing Mac and nearly getting

Mac and his future wife killed. Turned out Joe was the one taking bribes, stealing evidence and blackmailing fellow cops.

Eli had been a much younger detective then, naively blinded by loyalty to his veteran partner and unable to see the truth until it was too late. There was nothing naive left inside Eli anymore. And though *he'd* been the one to put the cuffs on Joe and had even, reluctantly, testified against him in court, several members of KCPD judged Eli guilty by association. He already triggered guarded suspicion whenever he entered a roomful of cops. He was Internal Affairs—the cop who policed other cops and held them accountable to the highest standards of their sworn duty. But there were some, like Captain Mitch Taylor, who seemed to take their distrust a little more personally.

Polite and professional as the captain might be, he wasn't here to make Eli feel welcome. "Will anything go into Banning's permanent file?"

"Everything points to a clean shoot." Eli chucked an empty creamer into the trash, stalling for privacy while two younger plainclothes officers waltzed in and grabbed a snack and a seat at the table on the far side of the break room. After a friendly scuffle over ownership of the remote control, they turned on the television and debated the merits of each show as they scrolled through the channels. "But any detective who's been involved in more than one previous incident deserves a thorough double check."

Captain Taylor watched and waited as well before adding, "I hear you're nothing but thorough."

"I do my job. I do it well." Except for the glaring error of not seeing his partner's corruption, Eli's reputation made it a fact, not a boast.

Taylor sipped his coffee, but there was no nonchalance in the steely set of his shoulders. "Just make sure you do it right. Banning's one of my best investigators. I don't want him stuck behind a desk indefinitely."

"Barring any glitch in the paperwork, you can have him on the streets by lunchtime."

The teasing scuffle on the far side of the room grew louder.

"Your mama's on TV again, Cartwright." The taller of the two young officers, a lanky smart-mouth with a shaved head, razzed his partner. "You know, if she wasn't old enough to be our mother, and I wasn't so damn handsome—"

"She *is* my mother," the shorter one articulated. "And you're not that good-lookin'. So put your eyeballs back…"

It wasn't their friendly, ribald banter that

caught Eli's ear so much as recognition of the name. *Cartwright.*

As in Shauna Cartwright, owner of the tempting backside pressed to his groin in the heat of gunfire, and the clean, subtle scent that had fueled some forbidden dreams last night. As in *Commissioner* Cartwright, the memory of whose laser-sharp tongue and official rank had rudely awakened him from his fitful sleep and sent him into the bathroom for a mind-clearing shower before dawn.

The commish had a kid? A *man* she'd raised? The family resemblance was there in the blond hair and the green eyes. But mother and son? No way. This stocky guy was twenty-five if he was a day. And she was... Hell.

Shauna Cartwright had to be a decade older than Eli. But the illicit beat of his pulse didn't slow with the knowledge.

Instead, it irritated him to discover he was attracted to a woman who was off limits for too many reasons to keep track of.

"You're not dating my sister, either," the young Cartwright warned to his fellow officer. "I've seen how you operate."

"A sweet guy like me?" Baldy feigned offense and saluted the television with his last bite of bagel. "I'm just sayin' she's—"

"Gentlemen." Taylor subdued them with a single word.

Eli's gaze slid to the TV, where a stock photograph of the commissioner graced the corner of the screen while the commentator related highlights of yesterday's robbery and double homicide at the Cattlemen's Bank's downtown office. Masking his interest behind a swallow of coffee, he listened for any mention of the *other* police officer who'd been on the scene and had taken down the alleged gunman with a shot to the knee.

But the focus was all about Commissioner Cartwright and how KCPD's top bureaucrat hadn't been behind a desk so long that she'd forgotten how to protect and serve the citizens of Kansas City when danger struck.

"Ah, c'mon, sir," the bald one was protesting. "We're on our fifteen."

"The morning briefing's in ten."

"Then we're on a ten-minute break?" Baldy tried to appease his boss.

"Better make it nine and a half so you can get front-row seats."

The two young officers echoed a dutiful, "Yes, sir."

"Front and center," Baldy added for good measure.

"Just be there." Taylor shook his head as though Cartwright and Baldy were the problem children of the Fourth Precinct. But there was no smile, indulgent or otherwise, when the captain took his leave of Eli. "Masterson."

"Captain."

"Whoa, man, there she is."

Eli pulled his gaze from Taylor's departure and tuned in to the television, too, to catch highlights from yesterday's news conference outside the Cattlemen's Bank.

A dramatic shot of two ambulances with their swirling red lights, and the bank's shattered front window formed a backdrop as Shauna Cartwright faced off against the press of reporters and photographers. The spotlight from several stations' television cameras bathed her even features in a cold, harsh glare. Her short hair formed a careless fringe about her cheeks and forehead, but there was an energy shining from her intelligent eyes and upturned chin that seemed to command the crowd—even more than the guarded stance of the man at her side. With the distinct, receding points of his dark brown hair, and the impeccable suit that masked the gun he wore at his waist, Deputy Commissioner Michael Garner was instantly recognizable.

Garner's dark, narrowed eyes scanned the

crowd as he inched closer to Shauna's shoulder. The man was expecting danger. An answering tension squeezed like a tight fist at the back of Eli's neck. Even through the television screen, Garner indicated that he sensed some kind of threat in the audience behind the camera. Maybe the man was protecting the office—not the woman. Maybe he was guarding KCPD itself from any questions that probed too far into events from the robbery/homicide.

Meanwhile, Shauna seemed unaware, or perhaps impervious to any potential danger as she fielded a barrage of questions.

She pointed to a dark-haired woman with a tape recorder. "Ms. Page."

The reporter wasted no time. "Having finally put a man on trial for the Baby Jane Doe abduction and murder, and now personally thwarting a bank robbery, do you feel you're settling into your new role as the head of KCPD?"

"You had to bring up Baby Jane." Officer Cartwright shot his wadded napkin at the TV screen, nailing the reporter's image. "Mom's had the job for almost a year now, toots. *She* had to take command before we finally got the damn case solved."

"Down, Tiger," Baldy raised a hand to calm his partner.

Young Cartwright crossed his arms over his chest and leaned back in his chair. From the most seasoned veterans to newbies like these two, the Baby Jane Doe murder case was a sore point that had plagued KCPD for over two years. A mutilated baby girl left in the city dump—unclaimed, unidentifiable. No parent had come looking for her; no clue had led to a real suspect. For months, the city had lived in fear for its children. Kansas City had mourned for the little girl whom no one seemed to miss, while they railed against the idea that such violence had come to their town. Through a charity drive headed by KCPD, citizens had raised money to give the girl a proper burial. But they still couldn't give her a name.

Closure was a long time coming for a weary police force with its reputation on the line. Eli knew firsthand there was often that one case which haunted a detective throughout his career. Baby Jane Doe's senseless murder was a case that had united the entire department, in frustration and sorrow.

But things had changed a few months ago. When Shauna Cartwright had been appointed to finish the term of the ailing commissioner, one of her first acts was to appoint a task force dedicated to the Baby Jane Doe investigation.

Kansas City finally breathed a little easier. The task force arrested Donnell Gibbs, a known pedophile, who'd confessed to the killing. The D.A.'s office was set to prosecute Gibbs for murder. Preliminary hearings in Gibbs's trial made news reports almost every night.

The story made good press, Eli supposed. But until Gibbs was in prison and the girl's story was laid to rest, there wouldn't be any real closure for Kansas City or KCPD.

Now there was one cool lady, Eli mused, mesmerized by the TV screen.

Without batting an eye, Shauna looked into the camera and diverted attention away from that hot-button topic by talking about the bank's two wounded security guards. "All of KCPD is keeping them in our prayers."

"Do you have the officers' names?" shouted another reporter.

"Not at this time. We're waiting, of course, until their families can be notified. The men are in good hands at St. Luke's Hospital, and I know their families will want to join them there."

"What about the two men who were killed? And the man you took into custody?"

The first detectable glitch in her control came when she rolled her shoulders as if she'd suddenly discovered a stiff muscle, no doubt a result of Eli's flying tackle. But she still made no mention of him.

Michael Garner had noticed the change, too, as he dragged his gaze from the audience down to the woman at his side. He whispered something to her, out of earshot from the camera. Shauna shook her head and crossed her arms in front of her, rubbing her palms along the sleeves of her white blouse as though nothing more ominous than a chill had shivered through her.

"We'll be sharing more information as it becomes available," she continued, ignoring Garner and her own discomfort. "In the meantime, we appreciate you honoring the guards' privacy and giving the doctors time to do their work. Thank you."

Before the news clip faded and the picture returned to the studio anchors, Eli zeroed in on the blood staining the commissioner's cuffs. The tension in his neck shifted and throbbed at his temple. He reached up and touched the two butterfly bandages that cinched the wound in his hairline.

Was that *his* blood? For all her cool, calm and collected facade, Shauna's hands had been surprisingly warm and urgent as she'd tended him. And her shapely body had shaken with fear, or perhaps simply an overabundance of adrenaline, when she'd been sandwiched between Eli and the floor.

"What the hell?"

Before Eli could quell his hormones' masculine response to the vivid memory of his boss's subtle feminine attributes, her grown son shot to his feet, swearing at the television.

"What?" Baldy asked, scrambling to catch up with his partner's mood swing.

"Did you see her clothes?" Cartwright tugged his cell phone from his pocket. "She didn't tell me she got hurt."

Eli drained the last of his coffee and observed the interchange, a very curious fly on the wall.

Mr. Comedy sobered up with a remark to calm his partner. "If it was serious, she would have told you. I heard she gave first aid to one of the downed guards. It's probably his blood, not hers."

Cartwright punched in the number. "Damn it, Coop, I'm calling her."

Baldy stood and tapped his fingers against his partner's fist. "Seth, your mom's a grown woman. And she didn't get the job she has just because she's pretty. She can take care of herself." He crushed his paper cup and made a neat, three-point shot into the trash can. "Besides, Captain Taylor will be waiting for us. Maybe he's going to finally brief us on that gambling case he wants us to work on."

"I guess you're right." Seth Cartwright paused to consider his partner's words, though his posture remained stiff and unyielding. "But after the meeting—"

"—I'll dial the number myself. C'mon."

Cartwright nodded. He flipped his phone shut and turned to follow his partner from the room. That's when he realized the six-four fly on the wall had never left the room. Cartwright's chest expanded with a deep breath as he glared at Eli. "What?"

Eli shrugged off the taunt. "Nothing. Just got caught up in the news report. The commissioner's your mother?" No response. Why didn't that surprise him?

Thick arms crossed in front of his wrestler's chest. "You're Masterson. That I.A. guy who's going after Detective Banning, aren't you?"

Going after? Hell. Would it kill anybody to say good morning around here? "How about, I'm the I.A. guy who's doing his job? Just like you. Banning has nothing to fear from me unless he did something wrong. Personally, I don't think he did."

"Uh-huh."

The visual standoff lasted a split second

longer before Seth's partner, Coop, called him to get his butt in gear and get to the meeting. With a dismissive nod, effectively telling Eli to mind his own business and keep any comments about Seth's mother to himself, the young officer strode from the room.

So Seth Cartwright was defensive about his mom. His partner's teasing was probably a mild example of the heat he took from his co-workers for being the head honcho's son. Probably had to prove himself a dozen times over to show he'd earned his spot on the force.

Of course, the young man had almost blown a gasket when he saw that blood. Maybe he wasn't defensive about his mom so much as he was defensive *of* the woman who'd raised him. Eli could have confirmed that none of the blood on the commissioner's clothes was her own. But it wasn't his place to say, nor was it his habit to make friendly reassurances.

Time to seek out Merle Banning and finish up the paperwork. Eli was anxious to clear his desk before *he* had to sit down and answer to a hearing about his involvement at yesterday's bank shooting. At least his name and face had been kept out of the media. Publicity generally meant even closer scrutiny. And while Eli had developed a knack for flying under the radar, he knew it was only a matter of time before one of his colleagues at I.A. called him into his or her office.

Eli hadn't even cleared the doorway when his cell phone rang. If he was a superstitious man...

Shaking his head, he pulled the phone from his belt and glanced at the number. Though he recognized the KCPD prefix, the number was unfamiliar. Hell. Why not? He *wasn't* superstitious.

He pressed the Talk button. "Masterson."

"Detective." The woman at the other end of the line breathed a sigh of relief before slipping into a more familiar clipped and confident mode. "It's Shauna Cartwright."

"Ma'am." His initial surprise at hearing her voice gave way to a misplaced pleasure, and more quickly to irritation. Shauna Cartwright had no reason to call him, except for business. And the only business they had in common was the damned paperwork for yesterday's robbery/homicide. He'd barely had a chance to scribble his notes, much less get them typed up. "If you're looking for my report, tomorrow's the earliest I'll be able to get it to you. And that's working on my own time."

Working off the clock certainly wasn't unheard of in his profession, but it would be damned annoying if he had to give up this particular evening to satisfy the boss's demands.

Not that Eli had anything more momentous planned than dinner with his sister Holly. But Holly was the one person with whom he could commiserate over their baby sister's plight.

After yesterday's hearing, complete with Jillian's sullen mood and accusatory glares, he and Holly would have plenty to hash out. Tough love sucked. But coping with an addict like Jillian had destroyed the whole warm-fuzzy-family thing among the three siblings long ago. While Jillian detoxed without any outside contact for two weeks, Eli and Holly needed to do some healing themselves.

Unfazed by his surly tone, the commissioner asked, "Can you come by my office this afternoon? I've already cleared it with Captain Chang. He gave me your direct number."

Running the request past his supervisor ensured cooperation, if not eager anticipation. Nothing like being master of his own destiny. Eli nipped the sarcasm and checked his mental calendar. "I can swing by about four-thirty if that'll work for you."

"That's fine. I'll have Michael take my last meeting."

"That anxious to get my report? Or are you going to lecture me about not following the chain of command again?"

Her volume dropped to a throaty whisper. "Please. I'd rather not discuss it on the phone. I need to see you."

Cryptic. Her hushed plea carved a delicate pinhole in Eli's defensive armor. Commissioner Cartwright hadn't struck him as a woman of mystery, but he couldn't help but be intrigued.

An image of the murdering Mr. Trench Coat's nearly opaque lenses trained down the barrel of his rifle toward Shauna Cartwright blipped through Eli's memory.

Forget *intrigued.* Tension twisted a knot at the back of his neck. "I'll be there at four-thirty."

BY QUARTER PAST FOUR that afternoon, Eli was sinking his oxfords into the plush silver carpet on the top floor of KCPD headquarters. The receptionist at the center of KCPD's administrative offices had offered him a seat, but Eli preferred the view at the row of windows facing into the heart of downtown Kansas City. At least he could see people moving outside.

KCPD's limestone tower wasn't the tallest building on the skyline. Originally built in the 1930s, the interior had been in a continuous state of refurbishing for the past six years. But it wasn't the new decor or updated technology or even the row of commissioners' portraits staring at his back from the long hallway that impressed him. It was the eerie quiet about the place.

There was an ominous weight to the air, a stuffy silence that lacked the relaxed comfort of a library or the creative intensity of a classroom of students taking a test.

Every floor in every precinct building he went into was a bustling hive of activity and purposeful noise. Machines. Conversations. Energy. Even the Internal Affairs division where he was based boasted more movement and warmth than this stylish tomb. Talk about your ivory tower.

It wasn't just the uniformed officers and security gates at each entrance that made the top-brass offices feel cut off from the rest of the world. The sound-dampening choices of carpeted cubicle walls and lined drapes played their part in the silence. As did the closed doors and deserted hallways. Even with the sun shining outside—deepening the reds and golds on the trees in the park below him—Eli felt isolated.

Waiting for his appointment with the commish was a bit like being summoned to the principal's office. Or going down to lockup at two in the morning to bail out a sister who was so zoned on booze and coke that she didn't even realize she'd been arrested.

Eli breathed deeply, trying to dispel the tension that particular memory triggered. He pulled back the front of his suit jacket and fingered the phone on his belt. Maybe he should call the treatment center to check up on Jillian. She wasn't allowed any personal calls during an initial probationary period, and then had to earn the privilege after that. But he could talk to one of her counselors or a nurse to see how she was settling in.

"Detective Masterson?"

Contenting his hands with rebuttoning his jacket instead of reaching for the phone, Eli greeted the receptionist with a nod. The steel-haired woman whose desk plaque had identified her as Betty Mills handed him a paper cup filled with coffee. Tepid from the feel of things. Bitter sludge that had sat in the pot all day from the whiff he got.

He still offered a polite "Thanks," not because the woman seemed to expect it or that he looked forward to drinking her gift. But a perverse sense of irony had him wondering if kindness could soften the plastic smile she wore like a badge on her stiff expression. Nope.

"It's inspiring to be in the company of such fine men, isn't it?" Betty stated with awed conviction. For a split second, Eli thought she was speaking in figurative terms, looking down at the miniature men and women outside—some in uniform, some in plainclothes—exiting down the concrete steps or entering the building for the start of their shift. But then he noted the angle of her gaze, toward the back wall and the row of portraits.

"There's a lot of history there," he agreed, wondering if her assessment included the commissioners who'd served in the 1920s and 1930s when there'd been suspicion of corruption among several government officials in Kansas City. But thoughts of corruption reminded him of Joe Niederhaus and soured what was left of his amiable mood.

"I've served with seven of them, you know. Either in the secretarial pool or as administrative assistant."

And he'd bet she'd worn that same smile through each administration. "You're very dedicated."

"I still miss working with Commissioner Brent. He was destined for fine things. Loved his sense of humor." Miss Plastic Face *got* humor? "Now it's all trapped inside him. But I know he's working hard to come back to us."

"I hope he recovers his health. I hear that rehabilitative therapy after a stroke is tough."

Betty straightened Brent's portrait with tender care, though Eli hadn't seen anything out of place. "He's a fighter."

The telephone buzzed on her desk and she left to answer it. Oh yeah, if she was in charge of the mood up here, no wonder it felt like such a mausoleum.

"Commissioner Cartwright will see you now."

Eli dumped his untasted coffee in the trash and strolled toward the bank of closed office doors. "Thanks."

But he paused when one of the double cherrywood doors opened and his I.A. supervisor, Garrett Chang, stepped out. Not the worst surprise of his life, but not a particularly good one. His captain's dark, almond-shaped eyes instantly sought him out and flashed a warning. Eli's mood shifted into grim. "This isn't gonna be good, is it?"

Chang shook his head. "I wouldn't want to be in your shoes."

This had to be about something more than a late report. Was one of the two dead men from the bank the cousin of a wealthy benefactor? Was someone suing the department? Was the lady commish p.o.'d because he hadn't jumped the instant she gave an order? Well, he damn well wasn't going to stand by while innocent...

"It's not what you think, Eli." Chang knew how his mind worked. "Whatever conspiracy theory is running around inside that head of yours, I promise, reality will be worse."

I'd rather not discuss it on the phone.

That vague sense of protective concern returned to mellow his temper as he remembered Shauna's call. Suspicion hardened him against the new, unknown threat. "What's wrong?"

Shauna Cartwright appeared in her doorway and answered the question herself. "Better let me tell him, Garrett."

"Right." Captain Chang stepped to one side, looking first to the commissioner, then Eli. "If there's anything I can do—for either of you— let me know."

The commissioner smiled, momentarily distracting Eli from his supervisor's mysterious offer. "Thanks. I'll keep you in the loop."

Chang took her outstretched hand, then reached over to shake Eli's. "Be good."

Was that a *mind your manners* or a *do your job* warning?

Garrett Chang departed without clarifying anything, and Eli began to feel the frustration of a man condemned to punishment for a crime he knew nothing about. Shauna Cartwright was no immediate help, either. She instructed Betty to hold her calls, gave her permission to leave at five o'clock, then ushered Eli into her office.

Though the decor in here was as uptown as the waiting area outside, soft touches of color added a subtle feminine warmth to the conference table and informal sitting areas. And was that...? Eli frowned at the nearly inaudible strains of a disco ballad playing from the suite's hidden speakers. Go figure. No canned elevator music or talk radio. There were signs of life in the ivory tower, after all.

But the lock twisted into place behind him, canceling out the unexpected sense of welcome.

The commissioner circled in front of him and held out her hand. "Thank you for coming."

Like he had any real choice. "Commissioner—"

"Shauna, please. In private, anyway." The jolt of her smaller hand sliding against his proved as surprising as her choice of music had been. She tightened her grip to keep him in place long enough to inspect the bandages at his temple. "I see you opted for the scarred and rugged look instead of sensible stitches."

"I'll live."

"I have no doubt you're a tough one." She led him to the sitting area, and then walked around her desk to a small kitchen area at the back. "May I get you a cup of coffee?"

The real thing? Or more of that stew Betty had served? He must have broadcast the questions telepathically because she grinned and pointed toward the door. "Betty may be as efficient as the U.S. Army, but she can't make coffee worth a damn. She insists she makes it the same way my predecessor, Commissioner Brent, always liked it. Makes me wonder if he dumped it down the sink and brewed his own when she went on break, too." She turned away to pour two mugs without waiting for his answer. "How do you take it?"

Apparently, there was no hiding a kindred caffeinated spirit. "With cream."

Though a sager suck-up would have asked a polite question about how the previous commissioner was recovering from the series of strokes that had incapacitated him, Eli dumbly watched the graceful movements of Brent's replacement.

Nice. She opened a tiny fridge beneath the counter and pulled out a carton of the real thing, whetting his taste buds in anticipation. *Very nice.* Regions south of his belt buckle stirred with a heated interest of their own as she bent over to replace the cream, and her navy gabardine skirt pulled taut across her backside.

Boss, Eli reminded himself, blinking and turning away.

His eyes fell on the computer printout with his name in bold print at the top, sitting at the center of her desk. That cooled his jets. She'd been checking up on him, reading the scattered commendations and more numerous complaints in his file, no doubt. How many partners had he gone through since Joe Niederhaus? Chang had finally given up trying to make him play well with others. The boss lady probably had something to say about that.

His gaze strayed to the pictures on her desk. Seth Cartwright with his arm around an attractive young blonde who shared a striking resemblance. The commissioner with a sopping, pony-sized Labrador retriever near a lake. A more formal photo of the commissioner, sandwiched between Seth and the same blond woman piqued Eli's curiosity further. Though there was no older man in any of the photos, no wedding ring on the hand that clutched the dog, there was no mistaking the sense of family in those photos. Eli had little in common with her world.

Maybe once. But camaraderie, teamwork, laughter, trust—those had been missing from his life for a long time. Since the tragic death of their parents, Jillian had turned to drugs. Holly had turned to work. And Eli had just turned...inward.

"Eli?"

He jumped like a rookie at the sound of his name.

"Sorry." She stood at his shoulder, close enough for him to smell the fragrant brew from the mug she pushed into his hands. Close enough to smell something more enticing than the coffee itself.

"Thanks." Eli hid his interest with a swallow of the beverage that burned his throat.

"Do you have any family?" she asked, glancing at the photos with a loving smile.

"Two sisters. You?"

"Two children. Seth and Sarah. Twins. Three, if you count Sadie." She reached over and stroked the dog's picture. "She's the only one still at home."

"Is there a Mr. Cartwright?"

"Yes. But we're divorced."

Damn. His pulse should not be racing any faster. Had to be all the caffeine in his system. "Sorry to hear that."

Soft green eyes sought him out over the rim of her cup, gauging the sincerity of his condolence. "It's his loss." The green eyes shuttered and she turned away, showing more willpower than Eli's sorry hormones could when it came to breaking the unspoken tension simmering between them. "It's my children's loss, actually. Austin has chosen to be a part of our lives only when it's convenient for him."

Her gaze was focused on the pictures again. No, they were focused toward some memory from the past, Eli thought.

"He could have been a good father if he wasn't such a…"

Such a what? Eli felt his body shifting forward, drawn to the sorrow that shaded her voice. But perhaps he had only imagined the vulnerability that had softened her posture. Because there was steel in the set of her shoulders when she turned to face him, and there was business in her smile.

"We have more important things to discuss. Have a seat, Eli." Oblivious to his misguided interest in her, the commissioner gestured to a sofa. "May I call you Eli?"

"In private." The smart remark was out before sense could stop it.

Instead of putting him in his place, she laughed. "Touché."

Eli unbuttoned his jacket and opted for a straight-backed chair at the conference table before he relaxed his guard any further and completely screwed up what was left of his day and career. "So, why am I here? I believe your exact words were *I need to see you.*"

"I like a man who's direct."

"I like a woman who's direct."

With a decisive nod, Shauna set down her mug and retrieved an unmarked file from her desk. "Just so you know, I've cleared this with Captain Chang."

"Cleared what? Is this about yesterday?"

"As a matter of fact, I asked him to lose any paperwork regarding your involvement in yesterday's shooting. For now, if anyone asks, we'll say the incident is under investigation. We can throw speculation onto the guards or even myself as the shooter."

Eli's gaze narrowed as she returned. "I've got nothing to hide. Taking down Mr. Trench Coat was a clean shoot. My report will say as much."

"Taking down Richard Powell was a hell of a shot. KCPD has had him on their person-of-interest list as a hired gun for several months now." She circled the table. "But forget your report. I need you on the job, not confined to a desk. As far as anyone outside this office knows, you weren't even at that bank yesterday."

"Why the cover-up?"

She pulled out a chair and sat across from

him, concentrating for a moment on placing the file folder just so on the table in front of her. But there was no hesitation in her expression when she looked up at him. "What I'm about to ask of you won't be easy. It won't make you very popular with your colleagues."

He inclined his head toward her desk. "You read my file. Does it look like *popular* matters to me?"

"Deep down inside—somewhere—it matters. That's why I've hesitated to recruit anyone for this assignment."

Ignoring the compassion she offered and denying any truth to her insight, Eli laced his fingers together and leaned onto the edge of the table. "What's the job, boss lady? What do you *need* me to do?"

He'd wanted direct. "Are you familiar with the Baby Jane Doe murder case?"

"I'm a cop and I live in Kansas City. So, yeah, I'm familiar enough." Relieved to have something to focus on other than the way Shauna Cartwright seemed to see a lot deeper beneath the skin than he liked a woman to, Eli eased back in his seat. "Murdered African-American girl. About a year old. I've heard the grisly details in the locker room. The body found separately from the head. Tossed in the dump. My sister's the M.E. who did the autopsy. There was no sign of sexual trauma, though the COD was physical abuse. Poor kid was too young to have dental records or finger-prints to ID her. I've followed the news stories. How people were keeping their own kids locked in at night, how they blamed the depart-ment for taking so long to arrest anyone. I know the D.A.'s office is hashing out the preliminary motions for Donnell Gibbs's trial right now."

"So you *are* familiar with the case." She sighed wearily, as if the details were far too familiar, maybe too personal, for her. "My first priority when I took over for Edward Brent was to put together a task force dedicated to the in-vestigation. Actually, it was Edward's idea, before his first stroke. He was afraid of civil un-rest. Lynch mobs. Untrained citizens arming themselves against a child-killer. I organized the plan, selected the investigators and put Mitch Taylor in charge. The task force gave me Donnell Gibbs."

Eli nodded. "Now the city's calmed down, the killer's on trial and we're all heroes here at KCPD again."

"I want to reopen the case."

A beat of silence filled the room.

"Are you nuts?" Putting Donnell Gibbs on trial

for Baby Jane Doe's murder had finally staunched the wound that had hobbled KCPD for more than two years. Even Eli could sense the city's massive sigh of relief. "Shauna, you can't—"

"I'm reopening the case." She ignored his accusatory slip of decorum and pushed the file across the table, offering Eli the most unpopular job in all of Kansas City. "And I need a man like you to do it."

Chapter Three

"You're giving in to anonymous threats?"

Shauna peeked over the top of her reading glasses to watch Eli set aside the last of the letters sealed in plastic evidence bags. His long, dexterous fingers tucked the pile into a neat stack before closing the folder.

"Yes, I want to find out who's sending these." She handed over the printouts of e-mails she'd received as well. Each and every message, from the vague comments expressing concern about the Baby Jane Doe case, to the perfunctory lists of mistakes KCPD had made in the investigation, to the most recent diatribes against the entire department's incompetence, had been signed with nothing more than a Yours Truly. "The sender might be able to provide a lead. But I'm reopening the case because I need to know that little girl's name."

Eli scanned a printout, then tossed it onto the table. "Ask Donnell Gibbs."

"He says he doesn't know."

"He's lying."

"I don't think he is."

"Why not?" Eli's prove-it-to-me gaze pierced the shadows falling across the conference table as the afternoon sun shifted into evening light.

Shauna imagined that that look alone could make a witness or suspect reconsider any lack of cooperation. She imagined that that look also kept well-meaning friends and serious relationships at arm's length. The cynicism in the smooth Scotch of Eli's eyes aged his handsome face. And she couldn't help but wonder how a smile, one that wasn't laced with mockery or distrust, would mellow his carved features and dark gold irises.

Still, any compassion she felt for his lone-wolf status was irrelevant. Any fascination she felt for his tall, lean body or rich baritone voice wasn't even allowed. Crossing her arms and rubbing at the skin chilling beneath the sleeves of her blouse was all she could do to assuage the empty ache inside her. There was another man out there—one far more mysterious and infinitely more dangerous—who demanded her attention.

"I might be the only person in all of Kansas

City who feels this way…but I don't believe Donnell Gibbs killed that girl." Shauna pulled off her glasses and got up, trying to warm the room by turning on a desk lamp and the overhead lights. "Gibbs confessed to killing her. But the man's a registered pedophile—and our Jane Doe wasn't sexually assaulted."

Eli stood as well, straightening his tie and rebuttoning his collar. "Maybe he got interrupted before he could do the deed. Or she screamed too loud and he had to shut her up before he got caught."

"She's younger than any of his other victims," Shauna pointed out.

"He had a need and was desperate. Maybe he discovered a twelve-month-old was too far out of his comfort zone, and that's why he killed her."

Shauna crossed her arms and tilted her chin. "You have an answer for everything, don't you."

"I'm just pointing out what the prosecution would argue. What every cop in this town is going to argue if you reopen this case." He picked up the stack of e-mails and held it out in his fist. "You should have reported this Yours Truly wacko the moment you got that first letter. Before it escalated to…" He shuffled through the papers to find one particular quote. "'Our children aren't safe. If your department can't get the job done right, Ms. Cartwright, then I'll do the job for them.'"

Shauna shrugged and moved to collect their empty mugs. "Do you have any idea how many complaints come through the commissioner's office? While we address all of them, we don't give credence to every disgruntled citizen who doesn't like the way we do business. Being frustrated with KCPD isn't a crime."

He slapped the letters down on the table beside her. "This isn't a complaint. It's a threat."

"I've read worse." Standing close enough to detect the clean, male smells on Eli's skin and clothes, Shauna had to crane her neck to look him in the eye. Lord, he was tall. Maybe not NBA size, but the lean cut of his waist and broad angle of his shoulders made him a towering figure.

"Such as?" he prompted, pulling her wandering focus back to the discussion at hand.

She wasn't reacting to anything Yours Truly had said, she reminded herself. There was a skewed logic about Donnell Gibbs's arrest that just didn't make sense to either the cop or the mother in her. She had to make Eli understand that. "Statistics say that the majority of sexual predators know their victims. They have some kind of contact prior to the attack. Gibbs claims she was a random abduction from the park."

"How does a one-year-old get to the park without…?" Eli paused, realizing he'd just slipped toward her side of the argument by stating another unresolved question in the case.

"Without anyone reporting her missing?" Zing. She'd scored a point in their verbal debate. "And how do you account for the signs of previous physical abuse? Gibbs claims he was only with her for forty-eight hours. That girl had a tragic life before Donnell Gibbs ever met her. If he really did."

"So there are holes in his story," Eli conceded, following her back to the kitchenette. "He has a couple of drug arrests on his record, too. Maybe the murder is related to that and not his predatory history. The task force report says his DNA was on the sheet the girl's body was wrapped in. That puts him at the murder."

"That puts him with the sheet. His DNA wasn't on the body."

Shauna set the mugs in the sink and shivered when Eli's sleeve brushed past hers. Damn. She was a grown woman with grown children. She had an entire police force under her command. She should be past this volatile-chemical-reaction-to-a-man phase in her life. So why were goose bumps prickling along her arms again?

Eli leaned his hip against the counter and faced her. "Are you *trying* to stir up a hornets' nest?"

Though his face was closer to her level, she still had to look up to make eye contact. "I'm trying to make sure we have the right man on trial. I don't want to give anyone in Kansas City a false sense of security."

Pulling back the front of his jacket, Eli propped his hands at his waist, unintentionally showcasing the chest that had shielded her from flying bullets and explosive debris. That chest was also radiating more heat than any other spot in her office. But he was regrouping to make a new argument, not issuing an invitation.

"That baby's unsolved murder was front-page news for over a year. Once Gibbs was arrested, people started letting their children play outside again. The men and women on that task force were handpicked by you. They got commendations. Hell, they could get the key to the city if they wanted." He hunched his shoulders, drawing his wounded face even closer. "You're going to raise a huge stink if you reopen this case and try to prove those ten men and women were wrong."

Shauna walked away, shaking off the inappropriate urge to gravitate toward Eli's abundant warmth. She felt cold again, but that

was merely a by-product of the strain she'd
been under. A hot bath and a good night's sleep
would boost her flagging energy. Trusting the
gut that had been honed by twenty-five years on
the force and summoning the strength that had
gotten her out of a debilitating marriage would
bolster her courage.

"I can deal with criticism, Eli. It's part of the
job description." Shauna stopped in the middle
of the room and turned to meet the challenge in
his eyes. "What I can't live with is the guilt."

"You're that certain the task force arrested
the wrong man?"

"After two years of nothing but panic and guilt
and broken hearts guiding us, I worry that we
were too eager to make this arrest stick. If the
wrong man's on trial, I want to know. An honest
mistake I can forgive—I will explain it to the
press and public—and I will back those officers
one hundred percent." She pulled back from her
soapbox with a deep, steadying breath. "But if any
man or woman on that task force skirted the facts
or forced Gibbs to confess, I need to know. I need
to find out who can tell me that little girl's name."

Eli nodded toward the stack of notes from
Yours Truly. "Personally, I think you should be
more worried about vigilantes than in getting
Gibbs off."

"I will not put an innocent man in prison or sentence him to death just to make the controversy go away."

Shauna held her breath, watching the pros and cons and consideration of facts play across Eli's face. He had to be evaluating how difficult such an investigation would be, and deciding if the grief he'd get from his fellow officers would be worth it. Damn, the man was thorough. "What if I say no to this assignment?"

"It's not a request."

"I see." Eli strolled off the distance between them. "So you asked Chang who the biggest hard-ass in I.A. was, and he came up with my name for this job."

"I asked Chang who his best investigator was. I could figure out the hard-ass part on my own."

His mouth quirked at the corner, as if her assessment of his character amused him. "You think I can take on the task force, the pride of KCPD and the sentiment of an entire city by myself?"

"I'll be working on the investigation as well."

Casting amusement aside, he dismissed that idea. "You're an administrator."

She'd never liked being dismissed. Pulling a ring of keys from her belt, Shauna picked up the file and opened her desk to lock the papers inside. "I've been a cop for a long time. I think I know my way around the job."

"Not this job, Shauna." He followed her, propping his fists on the opposite side of the desk and leaning over it. "You don't know what an I.A. investigation is like. You'll make enemies. You run the whole show. You need your people to stay loyal to you."

"I *have* enemies. Political ones," she amended, as soon as she realized she might have revealed more than she should. Shauna fisted her hands and countered Eli's stance. "Look, I can cut through red tape more easily than anyone on the force. I can get you any files you need, any transcripts—I can put you in contact with the D.A.'s office as well as Gibbs's attorney. But, like you said, I have to balance the department's reputation with the needs of the investigation. I can't go to my people and ask a lot of questions. Not that they'd share their secrets with the boss, anyway. That's why I need a front man to take the heat while I work behind the scenes."

"Someone who has a problem keeping partners and wouldn't automatically be linked to you?"

"Exactly."

She wasn't ashamed to reveal why she'd chosen him. It was the only tactical move that made sense without plunging the entire force into chaos. She needed a super-tough, super-smart SOB who could keep his head under the controversy that raising the ghost of Baby Jane Doe would surely generate. But as they stood there, almost nose-to-nose, her pulse racing and her breath coming in deep, uneven gasps, Shauna felt something inside her soften. Yearn. Need.

The air of warmth and strength that encompassed Eli reached out and touched her. Supplanted her own strength. Made her feel a lot more sheltered and a lot less alone in her quest for the truth.

"Please." Shauna shrugged off her unsettling emotions and reached deep inside to find the cool detachment and superior tone she was famous for. "Help me do this."

Eli released a huff that stirred a fringe of hair out of place across his forehead. "Do I have a choice?"

Her fingers itched to smooth the dangling lock away from his injury. But what she saw as an intimate caress he might see as mothering. She couldn't have one, and she didn't want the other.

"No. You're on my team now." Shauna had to step away to keep those traitorous feminine urges from upsetting the code of honor and decorum the job forced her to live by. A knock on her office door intruded, scattering both desires and resolutions.

"Shauna?" Michael Garner rattled the doorknob before his clipped voice grew more urgent. "The door's locked. Betty's gone home for the day. I know you're in there. Is everything all right?"

Glancing out the window, Shauna took note of the sun sinking like a giant golden orange ball on the horizon. She checked her watch. She and Eli had been hashing through the case for nearly three hours. "Oh, no."

"Shauna?" The deputy commissioner's knock shook the door.

Eli turned toward the door, his posture bristling. "What's he in such a tizzy about?"

A key scraped inside the lock. "I'm coming in."

Eli pulled back his jacket, sliding his hand to his gun.

The overprotective testosterone level on the top floor grew exponentially and Shauna roused herself to action. She laid a warning hand over Eli's, keeping the gun and the detective in place.

"I'm coming, Michael."

The door swung open as she reached it, and Michael blew in, snatching her by the arms and backing her up into the room. His eyes were dark with concern. "Why didn't you answer me?"

"You're overreacting—"

"This place is dead up here. I saw your light. I thought…" He looked past her and the worry on his face hardened with suspicion. In a subtle yet obvious move, he pulled her behind him, positioning himself between her and Eli. "What's he doing here?"

Groaning at his mistimed machismo, Shauna quickly extricated herself from his grasp. "Detective Masterson and I had a meeting. We were just wrapping up." She slipped back into completely professional address now that they had an audience again. "Have you two met?"

Introductions were brief, the handshake briefer. Michael looked from Eli's impassive expression back to her. "He's Internal Affairs. Is there a problem?"

She turned away from his question and spoke to Eli. "Will that be all, Detective?"

With a silent plea, she begged him to keep the purpose of their conversation secret. She didn't need the rumor mill getting ahead of, and possibly impeding, the investigation. Thankfully, she saw that those golden brown eyes could observe and understand without revealing anything. With a curt nod, Eli adjusted his tie and headed for the door. "I'll report as soon as I know

anything. Deputy Commissioner," he acknowl-
edged. He waited for Michael to move aside
before leaving. "Talk to you later, boss lady."

WHATEVER ENERGY Shauna had felt dissipated
as Eli strode down the hallway and disappeared
from sight. Strange that the touch of Michael's
fingers on her arm failed to generate even a
fraction of the heat she'd felt just bantering
words with Eli.

"*Boss lady?* That's practically insubordination. Tell me you called him in for a reprimand
of some kind."

Boss lady. Shauna allowed herself a hint of a
smile. At least Eli understood who was in
charge here. Though she felt that Michael's
concern was sincere, there was something more
controlling than caring in his loyal defense of
her. Letting him interpret her smile as a show
of thanks, she shrugged off his grip and crossed
the room to get her jacket and retrieve her purse.
"It was a personal meeting, Michael. I can't
disclose the details. How did the meeting with
the Chamber of Commerce go?"

"Fine." Though his mouth was set to push
for more information about Eli's visit, Michael
let her change the topic. "They want to do
something for Baby Jane Doe. I suggested

updating the playground equipment in one of the parks. They could post a plaque with the girl's name."

If they knew it.

"'Baby Jane Doe' on a plaque, huh? That's sweet that they want to remember her." Gesturing for Michael to exit first, Shauna turned out the lights and closed the door, locking it behind her. "I'd appreciate it if you'd continue to pursue that with them as KCPD's official liaison."

"You're stalling, Shauna." He fell into step beside her along the carpeted hush of the hallway. "Did we receive another threat from Yours Truly?"

Besides Eli and Betty, who handled the mail and might inadvertently compromise evidence or put herself at risk by opening one of YT's weekly harangues, Michael was the only person who knew of the threats against the department. And she'd confided to no one, not even Eli Masterson or her children, about just how very personal the messages were becoming. "No, I haven't heard from him recently."

"One of these days I'm afraid he'll put his threats into action. I thought maybe that's why you wanted me to deal with the Chamber and their memorial plans—that it was an uncomfortable reminder of his complaints about the case." Shauna quickened her pace, avoiding another hand on her arm. "Or are you still shaken from yesterday's shoot-out? I.A.'s not accusing you of anything, are they?"

While frustration screamed inside her head, Shauna kept her voice cool and calm. "I wasn't 'shaken' yesterday, Michael, and I'm not shaken by anything this evening. I'm just tired."

"So I shouldn't ask you to dinner then?"

He was a handsome man, in a mature-movie-star kind of way, and his PR skills made him an obvious boon to the department. But he couldn't take a hint. Even without the departmental rules and regs in placc, smooth-and-suave just wasn't her type. Not after Austin. But a good friend she could always use. So she smiled and gentled her rejection. "Can I tell you about the headache I have? A set of chills I can't seem to shake, too. I'm going home to some soup and aspirin and heading to bed."

"It's probably the aftermath from yesterday morning. Nerves are setting in now that you're starting to relax and put it behind you."

Behind her? "I understand that the older guard is still in critical condition. I won't put that holdup behind me until both men are out of the hospital, and I have a motive for Richard Powell's actions."

"He's lawyered up already, but we're working on him. Homicide's running the investigation. I've asked them to give me a daily update."

"Good. Any ID on the vics yet?"

"The guy in the sweatshirt was Charlie Melito, small-time hood for hire. Cleaning out the Cattlemen's Bank would have been his first successful job."

"Instead, it was his last unsuccessful one." As they passed the lineup of commissioners' portraits, the frozen stares gave Shauna the feeling of being watched. Scrutinized like a specimen under a microscope. She shrugged off the sensation she could do nothing about and concentrated on what she could handle. Work. "What about the banker?"

"Victor Goldsmith. We still haven't uncovered his connection to Richard Powell."

"Powell said he was following orders. If we could find out who hired him, I'd rest easier." If she could find out whether those mirrored sunglasses had targeted her specifically, or if she'd just been in the wrong place at the wrong time to wind up in his sights, she'd rest a hell of a lot easier. "Let me know as soon as you find out anything."

"Yes, ma'am. I won't let this be a blot on KCPD's record."

Unexplained motives. Anonymous threats. Wannabe suitors who should stay friends. It was no wonder Shauna was so overly sensitive to her surroundings. An uneasy twinge of suspicion slowed her steps as they reached the foyer.

The emptiness of the tiled area around the elevator wasn't completely unusual after hours. But something about the stillness nagged at her. The officer on duty at the information desk generally popped his head in to say goodnight if she was working late and was the last one on the floor to go home. But he would also leave to escort Betty down to the parking garage beneath the building if she asked him. Shauna frowned as Michael pushed the elevator's call button. "Did you dismiss Officer Tennant when you came up?"

Michael plunged his hands into his trouser pockets and assumed a casual stance. "He was gone when I got here. Why do you think I was so worried? I thought you were alone."

Being alone didn't bother her. The idea that someone might be watching her *while* she was alone did.

The rustling behind the stairwell door was probably a figment of her weary imagination. Or something as easily explained as a mouse. But imagining it twice?

Shauna turned toward the emergency exit. "What was that?"

Michael watched her with a blank expression. "What was what? Where are you going?"

She pushed open the stairwell door, hanging back in the foyer a moment until she was sure the landing was clear. Nothing. Just a yawning chasm of steel and concrete, angling round and round on itself. No one on the ladder to the roof, no movement on the stairs.

"Shauna?"

Sniffing the air, she detected the scents of dust and damp and the chemicals the cleaning staff used. Nothing out of the ordinary. But proof that her senses were playing tricks on her didn't make her breathe any easier. Shauna backed into Michael as she snapped the door shut behind her. "You didn't see anyone else up here?"

"No." Absorbing her tension, he glanced around, apparently deciding whether he should be alarmed. "Just your friend Masterson." Michael's hand settled at the small of her back, a guarded suspicion tensing his posture. "We never did actually see him leave the floor."

Shauna waved aside his suggestion, silently cursing her own paranoia. She had nothing to fear from Eli. "Believe me, the way he argues a point, he wouldn't be skulking in the shadows.

If he had something more to say, he'd be in our faces. It was probably a sound echoing from farther downstairs."

"Are you sure you're all right? You're acting kind of funny."

The number for the top floor lit up and the elevator opened. Shauna hurried to catch it and pushed the button for the parking garage. "I'm pooped, is what I am. I've been in meetings non-stop all day. I'll feel better once I'm home relaxing."

"Let me go with you."

"Michael. Please." She touched his arm to reassure him. She'd worry about the fine line they walked between friendship and whatever feelings he wanted from her later. "I just need some downtime. I'll be fine."

"You're sure?"

"Positive. But thanks for caring."

"All right." The devilish points of his receding hairline softened as he smiled. "But I'm walking you to your car."

Shauna laughed at his stubbornness and relented, knowing it was easier to go along with Michael Garner than to say no. And knowing some company—even a meticulously attentive coworker like Michael—was better than none.

Because, despite any rational explanation to

the contrary, she hadn't imagined those footsteps scuffling behind the door.

"So, WE GO straight from 'how've you been?' to 'let's talk about an old autopsy case'?" Holly Masterson downed half her iced tea and signalled the waiter for a refill. "I thought I'd at least get my food before we ran out of things to talk about besides work."

Eli had to gauge the expression in his sister's hazel eyes to determine whether that was teasing or a comment on his social skills. Looked like a little of both. "Sorry, Holl. How *have* you been?"

"Fine. I've taken up running again." He could tell that by the trim fit of her clothes. "It gets me out of the lab when I need to."

"How have you gotten along since Jilly's sentencing?"

"Why do you think I need to get out of the lab?" Holly's smile faded and he could see the lines of strain bracketing her mouth. "I suppose you're still keeping it all bottled up inside, snapping at people or cracking wise when an emotion tries to slip through?"

"Is sarcasm the only habit you picked up from me growing up?"

Holly laughed, and for a split second they

were kids again—before the plane crash had killed their parents, before Jillian's wild-child escapades and their futile efforts to help her had fractured what was left of the closeness they'd once shared. "No, big brother." She toasted him with a fresh glass of iced tea. "I also learned how to take down any guy who gets too fresh with me—not that they're lining up—and I learned that you would always be there when the chips were really down."

"Hell." Eli reached for his beer, uncomfortable with the subtle expression of gratitude and praise. "I haven't been there for anybody lately."

Holly shook her head, stirring her short, dark hair. "Let's see... who registered for legal guardianship of his two teenage sisters so that the three of us could stay together? Who played tough guy at Jillian's first intervention—"

"—which didn't take—"

"—And who took a second job while he was in school so we could keep the house?"

"We all worked." He insisted on sharing the credit.

"You posted bail after Jillian's last arrest and testified on her behalf at the trial."

"So did you."

"And how many times have you called the

Boatman Clinic to see how Jillian's rehab is going?"

"You know we can't contact her for two weeks."

Holly focused in on his belt. "How many times have you had your fingers on the phone *wanting* to check on Jillian?"

It was Eli's turn to shake his head and slip his sibling a wry smile. "Very perceptive, Dr. Phil. And how many times have *you* wanted to call?"

Holly's smile widened. "About as many times as you have."

Some of the guilty tension inside Eli relaxed. "Are we ever going to get over worrying about her?"

"I don't think you get over worrying about people you love."

Eli reached across the table to touch Holly's hand. "I worry that I don't check in on you enough."

She turned her hand to squeeze his. "We're both adults. We have demanding jobs that take a lot of our time and energy. We lead our own lives."

"I just don't want you to think that…you know…"

"That Jillian's the only sister you care about? You invited me to dinner, right?" Holly winked. "And you're paying, aren't you?"

"It's definitely my treat. To spend time with you," Eli added, blending his compliment with sarcasm, just as she had done earlier.

But Holly stopped smiling as she pulled away. "You still can't say it, can you?"

He wouldn't feign ignorance and pretend he didn't know which three words Holly was talking about.

"I love you, too, big brother. Your actions have always shown me how much you care. And if Jillian's head were clear, she'd see it, too." She toyed with the condensation rolling down the side of her glass. "But you know, I think being able to tell a person you love them is as important to you as it is to them. You're admitting it out loud. Owning that feeling. Taking responsibility for it."

"You're a forensic pathologist, right? Not a psychiatrist?"

Holly grinned at his deadpan refusal to let her probe any deeper into his emotions. She sat back as the waiter arrived with their dinner. "All right. Enough of the mush. What do you want to know about the Baby Jane Doe case?"

Chapter Four

Shauna dragged her feet across the parking garage at St. Luke's hospital, carefully assessing that hers were the only footsteps to be heard.

A second straight day of meetings, ending with this after-dinner visit with the two injured guards and their families, left her brain cranking out a to-do list that never seemed to end. But the long days had dulled her body to all but the single goal of getting home and getting comfy—whichever she could manage first. If the concrete floor weren't stained with oil leaks, old gum and the sticky residue of a discarded soft drink, she'd pull off her high heels and walk to her car barefoot.

Not that she didn't appreciate a pretty shoe. But with each year on the force, the days seemed to get longer. Or maybe it was each new layer of responsibility added on with each promotion that made her long for hot baths, foot massages and snuggles with Sadie to ease away the strain of the day.

Responsibilities like listening to the father of the young guard with the lacerated face and eyes who expected an answer when he asked why his son had been hurt. Who expected justice to be delivered on his son's behalf. Responsibilities like knowing someone had such disregard for a little girl's life that he'd throw her away with the trash. Like fearing the children of Kansas City weren't as safe as their parents thought because the real killer was still out there.

A killer who taunted Shauna as though getting away with murder was a game he wanted her to play. And if she couldn't beat him, there'd be a horrible price to pay for losing.

This was the kind of day that made everything from her feet to her heart ache. The kind of day that made her question whether Edward Brent had been in his right mind when he'd scribbled that memo recommending her as his successor. That had been after his first stroke, while he could still write. Before the other strokes had hit and he'd been incapacitated and she was thrust into the job. She'd gone from negotiator to executive advisor to commissioner in the span of two years. And she was tired.

But just as when her husband had cleaned out

their savings and lost their family home on the promise of the next "sure thing," there was nothing Shauna could do but hold her chin up and move on. Her own needs had to be secondary to the job at hand. She'd had children to raise and provide for back then. Now she had an entire city to look after.

A pair of aching feet and a stomach with nothing but worry to fill it wouldn't stop her from doing what needed to be done.

The night sky filtered in and shrouded her vision, despite the yellowish glare of the garage lights. With her purse tucked beneath her arm and her keys gripped firmly between her fingers, Shauna picked up the pace and strode with purpose toward her car. She could drive through somewhere to grab a bite to eat, and still have time to reread more of the task force's report before hitting the tub and trying to relax enough for a decent night's sleep.

Relax? Ha. Not since she took this job. Not since the messages had started.

Her steps stuttered when she heard a car squealing around the garage's sharp corners. She paused beside a concrete pillar. Was the car racing toward the street exit? No. It was coming up, coming closer. Grinding through the gears, tormenting the suspension. She braced one hand against the clammy concrete, breathing harder with the sense of disaster barreling toward her.

It was on the level below her now, picking up speed in the straightaway. Braking and screeching up the ramp. She caught a glimpse of blue fender veering around the corner before she dove behind the pillar and prayed for solid engineering.

Ignoring the burning pain as concrete scraped off a strip of her knees, Shauna curled into a ball and braced for the impact, swearing when another woman might have screamed. But the driver raced on by in a blur of sky-blue, never swerving, never slowing, never looking back to see how close he'd come to hitting her.

"That son of a…" She scrambled to her feet and ran out from her hiding place into the pungent aftermath of burnt rubber and spent gas. "Idiot!"

Shaking off the remnants of self-preserving adrenaline, Shauna wondered if it was worth the bother to try to get an ID from the two numbers she'd deciphered off the license plate. She glanced down at her bloody knees and ruined hose and swore. She was relieved that it hadn't been a personal attack, that the veiled messages of the past few weeks hadn't progressed into violence. But it irritated the hell out of her that fear for her own safety had been her first reaction. That she *had* believed she was under attack.

That *he* could make her afraid.

"You're losing it," she chastised herself, hurrying toward her parking space, heedless of sore feet and turbulent thoughts now. The blue sedan was probably a kid out joyriding, or a desperate family member using speed to relieve the stress of worrying about a hospitalized loved one. "There's absolutely no reason why…"

"Shauna!"

Shauna jerked, halted, slipped her hand into her purse and wrapped her fingers around her gun. Damn it, she *was* spooked.

"KCP—" was as far as she got.

"What the hell was that? Are you all right?" A tall figure emerged from the shadows and jogged toward her Lexus. Broad shoulders took shape. Dark gold eyes narrowed as Eli Masterson stepped into the light, blocking her path. "First Powell, now this? I got the make and plate, but I couldn't get a good look at the driver. Dammit, you're hurt." He knelt at her feet.

"Get up!" On emotional overload, Shauna smacked the first thing she could reach, which happened to be his shoulder. The immovable object simply absorbed her frustration, shredding the last of her self-control. "What are you doing here? Spying on me? Why aren't you chasing down that jerk and giving him a speeding ticket?"

Ignoring both the outburst and the subsequent apology, Eli inspected her wounds and announced she'd be wanting soap and water and a couple of aspirin for the aches that would surely follow. Then he stood and backed away. His breathing had regulated far quicker than her own. "I did give chase. I know you think I'm good, but even I can't catch a speeding car on foot." He wasn't joking and he wasn't retreating. He snatched a note off the windshield of her car and waved it in her face. "You didn't tell me this was personal."

Oh, God. Fear and temper vanished in a heartbeat and she grabbed the paper from his hand. "No, I didn't."

Take the hint. Let it go.

She turned away to inspect the wrinkled page. The plain type was big enough to read without her glasses.

Ms. Cartwright,
I said you was wrong about Baby Jane Doe and you didn't lissen. Peeple who make mistakes have to pay for them. Your the

only cop I see talking about it, so I guess it has to be you.

Donnell Gibbs is a stupid man, and I expect he's guilty of something. But not this.

I said I'd be watching to make sure you do your job right.

Come find me.

Before I have to come find you.

Yours Truly

Even with typos, the message was clear.

"Damn." Shauna automatically went on guard, scanning the silent cars and empty drive around her. She even checked the bright lights of the hospital windows across the street, searching for any curious voyeur or telephoto lens that might be trained on her.

Eli's voice droned behind her. "I've been here twenty minutes. Scouted the area. Whoever left that note isn't here anymore."

So he was a mind reader. No, he was a note reader. Trouble wasn't watching; it was right here beside her. Carefully folding the note into her purse, Shauna skirted around Eli. She needed to get out of here.

"This isn't the first time he's contacted you, is it?" Shauna opened the door, but a bigger hand was there to push it shut. "Is it?"

She spun around, pressing her hips against the car to force distance between them because the big galoot wasn't budging. "You're familiar with insubordination, aren't you, Detective?"

"You're familiar with 'suicide by cop,' aren't you, boss lady?" His lips danced before her eyes, articulating each word. "'Come find me?' He's too big a coward to turn himself in, but he's got no problem terrorizing you into tracking him down." Eli braced a hand on the roof of the car beside her, leaning close enough that his body heat radiated between them. "Don't play his game. Report him."

"It's just a bunch of talk."

"Bull. That's why you jumped like you'd been shot when I ran up a minute ago. 'Cause you're scared of *talk*."

"I don't respond to threats. From him or you." Shauna flattened her palm at the center of Eli's tie and shoved, barely forcing an inch more space between them. "Trust me. I know this is no game. He might be Jane Doe's real killer, or he might just be a crackpot on a power trip. Either way, I'm not going to hunt him down and grant him his wish. I'm not going to let him call the shots. If he's our murderer, I'll prove it and he'll go on trial in Gibbs's place. If he's not, then he's not a priority right now, and I will deal with him once—"

"—he's made himself a priority." She was pushing against a breathing brick wall. "You can't ignore him, or he'll bring the battle to you. You're a trained negotiator. You know that when a perp decides getting blown away is the punishment he deserves, other people get hurt. It escalates into a hostage situation, or he shoots first." Eli pressed into her bracing hand. The rhythm of his breathing and the hum of his voice vibrated through her fingers and palm, tingling up her arm and waking something deep inside her. "If the guy has a death wish, gunning for the commissioner is a damn sure way to get KCPD on his tail."

The intensity of those golden brown eyes skittered along the same path his voice had taken. Her temperature rose, even as the autumn air cooled the night around them. She should be shivering, but all Shauna felt was raw, charged heat.

Anyone driving past would think they were a couple stealing a private moment. Standing nose to chin, their gazes locked. Her fingers clutched around his tie, holding him close—his arm, wrapped around her shoulder, shielding them from curious eyes.

Instead, they were locked in battle. Two strong wills, talking business, not pleasure. Fighting, not flirting.

She'd embarrass herself if she confused the two. Shauna had to be a boss, not a woman. She had to remember that Eli was a younger man more interested in making a point than in scoring points.

She needed to hear the words. Interpret the innuendo. Ignore the heat that surged inside her and quit craving the sense of shelter his tall form and tough hide provided.

"You think Richard Powell was there for me at that robbery, don't you?" Matching wits with Eli demanded concentration. Besting him demanded something more. "I appreciate your concern for my safety, but if Powell wanted me to shoot him, why wear a Kevlar vest? If that maniac driver wanted to provoke me into pulling my gun just now, why have such lousy aim? Believe me, you're the only thing I've been tempted to shoot lately."

A little logic and a hint of humor eased the tension beneath her hand, and a hint of a smile played at the corners of his mouth. "All right. So Yours Truly isn't Richard Powell, and it probably isn't that guy in the Buick. We don't know who he is."

"Right."

Eli should have backed away. Shauna should have pushed. Neither of them moved.

"But he sure as hell knows who you are. He knows the car you drive. He knows your itinerary—or he's able to follow you without being detected."

Eli was killing the mood that shouldn't be brewing between them in the first place. "A lot of my appearances are public knowledge. And I promise to do a better job of looking over my shoulder."

"Why do I get the feeling you've been doing that for a while already?" Couched in that soft, rumbly whisper, Eli's deep voice completely short-circuited whatever resolve Shauna had left in her.

For a few precious seconds, she wasn't the commissioner. She wasn't a cop. She wasn't a mom. She was just…a woman. Her pulse tripped along in her veins and she felt feminine, vulnerable, needy. And when the rough pad of Eli's thumb wiped a smudge from her cheek, she leaned into the caress. He opened his palm, tunneled his fingers into her hair.

"This can't be happening." She said the words she knew she should, but her brain was disconnected from the need inside her.

"I know." Eli's voice sounded just as constricted as hers.

He brought his other hand up to frame her

face, to tilt her mouth up toward his. He brushed his thumb across the curve of her bottom lip and studied her breathless reaction. She felt hot. Unbearably, inordinately hot. Even in the early days with Austin, before the debts and shame and scandal, she'd never reacted like this. So fast. So completely. To just a touch. A look. Her fingers curled deeper at his chest, catching silk and crisp broadcloth and the solid muscle underneath in her needy grip.

He leaned in.

"Shauna…" Years had passed since she'd kissed a man in passion. She hadn't known how much she wanted—needed—to be touched by passion. Desire had never slipped past her control like this. He blinked slowly and halted his descent. "What else has this guy said to you?"

There would be no kiss. Passion crashed and burned and rational thinking fought to resume its rightful place.

"Nothing." Her tongue felt dry in her mouth.

Eli arched a dark brow. Yeah, he believed that one.

His hands on her face seemed more of an embarrassing trap than a sheltering caress. She swallowed hard, regaining more of her voice. "Just that he's watching. This is only the third personal note in three weeks."

"Only?"

Forcing discipline back into her body, she flattened both palms against his shoulders and pushed. "Is there a reason you're here, butting your nose into my business, Detective?"

Detective was as effective as a slap in the face. Conceding that things had gotten too personal between them, Eli swept his hands out to either side of his body and backed away. Cynicism returned to the set of his eyes and mouth. "Yes, ma'am."

Missing his heat and the heat he stirred inside her, a suddenly cold Shauna hugged her arms around her middle and waited for an explanation.

He smoothed his tie until it looked as though she'd never had her hands on him. "I wanted to let you know I'm ready to start asking questions. I spent the day looking at Dwight Powers's case. By the way, the D.A.'s office isn't too thrilled that you're having second thoughts about Gibbs's guilt."

"Dwight Powers is more dedicated to justice than any man I know. Besides, he owes me one. He'll cooperate."

"Fine. I'll start digging tomorrow. But I want access to the task force members' personnel files before I start interviews. See if there are any personal issues that might make them vulnerable to outside influences."

"I'll have them for you by tomorrow afternoon."

"Pick them up at your office?"

"Fine."

"Be sure you take care of those knees." It was a statement of polite concern and served as a good-bye. Eli headed to the SUV she assumed was his, and she exhaled a silent sigh of relief tinged with regret. But Shauna barely had her door open when he strode back to her car. "You didn't even have your cell phone on to call for backup if you needed it. I had to call Deputy Commissioner Garner to find out where you were. You need to be more careful."

Just like that, fatigue vanished and the verbal battle was on again. "The executive committee is aware of Yours Truly's threats to KCPD."

"What about your own safety?"

"I suppose Captain Chang has reprimanded you about taking liberties with a person's privacy?"

Eli pointed to the windshield. "Hey, the note was right there in plain sight."

Shauna shook her head. "What am I going to do with you?"

The question landed like a loaded grenade in

the still air, filled with all the sexual overtones that had awakened her dormant hormones and simmered between them. But Eli was smart enough to keep any innuendo to himself. "Let me do my job. I can handle whatever crap the task force gives me. I'll try to keep it an I.A. affair and keep you out of it as much as I can. But…you have to report the personal threats."

"No."

"Tomorrow, Shauna."

"You can't give me an order."

"Maybe not, but I can try to drill some sense into you." He raked his fingers through his hair, knocking that independent strand out of place. She curled her fingers into tight fists to keep from reaching up to straighten it. "It's been a while since I've had a partner. But I'm pretty sure that anything that's a danger to you is a danger to me and to our investigation."

She glared at him. "I don't want an armed guard watching over me, and I don't want my movements restricted. I can't do my job that way. Being a woman is already a strike against me in a lot of people's books. I can't afford to show any weakness, or it will completely undermine my authority with both the public and the department."

"If another cop had been threatened, you'd do something about it," he argued.

"There isn't another cop in charge of the whole show." She was done. Despite her personal, mixed-up craving to get closer to Eli, as commissioner, she couldn't stand here debating the issue. "Goodnight."

She thanked him perfunctorily when he held the car door open for her, and pretended the small chivalry didn't please her. He waited for her to lock her car and start the engine before he climbed into his own vehicle.

When she reached the second stoplight and he pulled up behind her for a second time, Shauna turned on her cell phone and called him. She watched him pick up in her rearview mirror. "What are you doing, Eli?"

"Making sure you get home."

"That's not the job I asked you to do."

"I'm off duty." The light changed and he trailed her through the Plaza onto Brush Creek Boulevard. "Following pretty women in snazzy cars is a hobby of mine."

"You can't call me pretty. Read your sexual harassment handbook."

"Just stating a fact, ma'am. You wouldn't catch me making a pass at the boss."

Shauna wanted to laugh at his gentle teasing. Even couched in sarcasm, she hadn't been flirted with in a long time. Or maybe it was his relentless concern that made her feel a little less frightened and alone tonight. Hmm. Maybe *she* should reread the harassment handbook. "Go home, Eli. This guy hasn't had the guts to show his face yet. He won't show it now."

"Trust me. He will. His threats have gone from departmental to personal. He says he's already watching. The next step is to make contact. You might not even know it, but he'll be there. And the moment you drop your guard is when he'll make his move."

The truth was a chilling thing. But she didn't want Eli to know how much hearing it out loud rattled her. "Hang up or I'll have to pull you over and cite you for using your cell phone while driving."

"Do that." Warmth filtered in at the wicked smile in his tone. The presumptuous SOB was still on her tail as she turned toward home. "I'll just file a complaint with the commissioner's office."

"HEY, MOM! Sadie alert!" Sarah Cartwright popped out the front door a step behind the long-legged Lab who bounded across the yard to greet his mama.

Shauna willingly braced for the excited welcome home from the spoiled-rotten puppy with the big brown eyes and loving tongue. "How's my good girl? How's my very best good girl?" Sadie leaped at the praise, allowed herself to be scratched behind the ears and petted on the flanks. Then she loped off to inspect the black Chevy Blazer that had pulled up to the curb behind Shauna's Lexus.

For the moment, Shauna ignored Eli's SUV and asked about the unexpected but welcome sight of the familiar car and truck parked in her driveway. "I know I didn't miss anyone's birthday. What are you and Seth doing here tonight?"

Sarah reminded Shauna of the woman she'd been twenty years ago. Not just in the slender build and blond ponytail, but in the bright eyes and easy smile that declared she was ready to take on the world—and aimed to do so. As always, Shauna prayed that her daughter's journey through life would be easier than her own had been.

Slipping off her shoes and carrying them by the heels, Shauna hurried to the front porch to trade hugs. "Hey, sweetie. Is everything okay?"

"As far as I know. What happened to you? You look like one of my fourth-graders on the playground." Sarah glanced beyond the circle of light shining from the front porch to where Sadie was greeting Eli. "And who's the guy?"

So much for guarding the place. Sadie barked in delight when Eli ruffled her fur, and gleefully gave chase when he tossed a stick. The fact that Sadie had taken a shine to grumpy Mr. Masterson shouldn't mean anything. Sadie liked anybody who'd play with or pet her.

"She's shedding like a big bear before she gets her winter coat," Shauna tried to warn Eli in an attempt to discourage him from hanging around any longer than necessary. "You'll get gold hair all over your suit."

Eli strolled up the hill and Sadie lumbered up beside him, begging to chase the stick again. Eli obliged and Sadie took off. "I don't mind. We used to have dogs growing up. I miss them."

Seth opened the screen door and joined them on the porch. "Hey, Mom." He kissed her cheek and hugged her tightly.

Shauna hugged him right back. "What's going on with you two?"

"What's he doing here?" Seth drilled Eli with a warning look.

"Mom has a friend." Sarah extended her hand and a smile. "I'm Sarah Cartwright."

"Eli Masterson." So…Mr. Sarcasm *could* manage a friendly grin if he wanted to. "Good to meet you."

But Shauna was just as interested in Seth's

bristling reaction. "You know Detective Masterson?" she asked.

"By reputation." Seth stepped down to Eli's level. Seth was short by Cartwright standards, a good six inches shorter than Eli, but his brawny wrestler's build could intimidate if he chose to. So why was he choosing now to play tough guy? "You were in the break room yesterday."

But Eli didn't intimidate. "Did I give Detective Banning a fair enough deal to suit you?"

Seth reluctantly conceded to an issue that would remain a mystery to Shauna. "Banning had no complaints. So I can't, either." But agreement didn't mean welcome. "What brings you to the house?"

"*My* house, junior." Shauna chided him with a stern but loving look. "*My* guest. I had a bit of an accident in the parking garage," she vaguely explained. "Detective Masterson followed me to make sure I got here safely, that's all."

"Accident?" Seth shifted his worry to her. "Are you hurt? Is the car all right?"

"Fine on both counts," she reassured him, squeezing his arm. She turned to Eli to shake his hand as any two professionals would do, to thank him and send him on his way.

But making contact proved to be a tactical error. Apparently, even something as innocuous as a handshake between them charged her pulse with that forbidden sizzle which disrupted her good intentions. Eli's long fingers folded around hers. The callused pads of his fingers brushed across her knuckles like a caress, and she couldn't help but recall how gentle those strong hands had felt on her face.

Get it together, Shauna! She quickly pulled away, remembering where she was, whom she was with and how she was supposed to act. She didn't want her children questioning why an Internal Affairs officer had followed her home. And considering Sarah's wink-wink notice of their tall, dark and cynically handsome guest, Shauna didn't want them questioning anything else, either.

"As you can see, the troops are here. I'm in good hands," Shauna said. "Thank you."

"You're welcome." *Keep it professional,* she silently begged. Eli delivered. "Ma'am."

"Good night, Detective."

"'Night, boss lady."

Shauna didn't know whether to grin or protest at the sly use of the irreverent nickname that was beginning to feel like a coded…endearment?

No, no, no! Her rusty signals were getting crossed. She needed to call him on it.

But he was already striding to his car, the dog trailing behind him with her stick.

"Sadie! Here, girl." Seth's shrill whistle prevented Shauna from saying anything. By the time Sadie had launched herself back into the house, Eli was in his Blazer, and the black vehicle had disappeared into the blacker night.

Shauna should be feeling relief. But the tension that left with Eli was replaced by a different kind. One where she was alone again, and unseen eyes were watching.

"Mom?"

But she *wasn't* alone.

"Long day." That was all the explanation it took to erase the frown on Sarah's face. With Seth's mood still curiously dark, Shauna linked arms with her son and daughter and urged them after Sadie. Inside the privacy of her newly built Tudor home on the southeast edge of Kansas City, Shauna could shed the rules and regs that governed her professional life and simply relax and be a mom. "So—tell me what this is about. You two don't both show up in the middle of the week unless there's something going on."

"I wanted to have a family meeting." Seth tempered the seriousness of that announcement by adding, "I missed dinner tonight, and

I figured your leftovers would taste better than Sarah's—"

"Hey!"

"—so she agreed to meet me here so I could talk to both of you at once."

"Family meeting, huh?" Shauna led them to the kitchen table where they'd sat together and shared meals and conversations on and off for the twenty-six years she'd been blessed with her twins. The table was one of the few things that hadn't been pawned or repossessed or auctioned off during her marriage to Austin, and it remained the heart of any Cartwright gathering. "Make yourselves at home. Let me change out of these clothes and then we'll see what falls out of the fridge."

Two hours later, the family mood was much grimmer by the time the three of them, along with Sadie, were washing up the dishes.

"I might not be able to check in as often as I'd like," Seth explained, setting the last plate in the cabinet. "But I'll bow out of the assignment if you guys need me."

He was referring to her accident at the garage, to Eli's visit, to the strains and demands of her job as commissioner. She couldn't let Seth's overdeveloped sense of being the man of the family, in place of his absent father, keep him from doing *his* job. She'd known this day was coming, that undercover work had been a goal of Seth's from the day he'd walked through the police academy doors.

"Don't be ridiculous," she reassured him with a conviction the mother in her couldn't quite feel. "We'll be fine. Why does Captain Taylor think you're the man for this undercover assignment?"

"Coop and I volunteered. We're vice squad now, Mom."

Sarah gathered the damp towels and hung them on the stove handle. "What does that mean, exactly? Vice. Are you going to be going after prostitutes? Drug dealers?"

"I'll be working down at one of the casinos on the river."

Shauna sank into a chair. Even Sarah's sisterly teasing stopped.

"Gambling?" Shauna whispered. She could quote statistics on the exponential rise in crime since the casinos had opened. Burglaries and muggings. Scams. Illegal gaming. Murder. But it was a vice that had touched her family much more personally. The addiction had destroyed her marriage and turned her children's lives upside down.

"Right now, I just got hired on as a bouncer for one of the clubs." He took her hand and sat in the chair across from her. "Would it make you feel any better if I told you we're investigating possible underworld connections? I may never have to get close to the tables at all." Shauna rolled her eyes. He knew that motherly glare. "I didn't think so."

"I knew I hated you becoming a cop." Sarah walked up and gave her brother a hug.

He pulled her onto his knee and squeezed her tight. "Hey. I'll be all right. Coop and I have been training for this. And you know I know my way around the casino—as many times as I've been in there to pull Dad out."

Shauna's heart squeezed with guilt. It was bad enough when her ex hit their children up for money. But if Austin Cartwright had done anything to jeopardize Seth's safety... "Does this assignment have anything to do with your father?"

"You know I can't go into detail, Mom. The less you know, the safer you and Sarah will be."

There *was* something more. But Seth couldn't say. And she couldn't ask. She couldn't even call Mitch Taylor and demand what danger he'd placed her son in. It would be a terrible abuse of her power and an even worse embarrassment to Seth.

When Seth was ready to leave, Shauna

sucked it up and told him how proud she was of him and how she trusted his ability to think on his feet and do his job well.

"My reputation's gonna go to hell pretty fast, but that's part of the plan." At the front door, Seth hugged his mother and sister both, and gave them each a kiss. "I'll check in when I can. And just remember, no matter what you see or hear, I love you. You three girls…" he included Sadie with a rub along her muzzle, "keep out of trouble and stay safe while I'm gone."

"We should be saying that to you."

"So say it."

Shauna wrapped her arms around Seth and hugged him tight. The tears that stung her eyes were gone before she finally released him. As director of the police department, she wrestled with the knowledge that the men and women who worked for her put their lives on the line every day. She cared about their safety, felt responsible for the risks they took. But this time she was sending her own son into battle. "Keep your eyes open and stay safe. Watch your back. I love you."

ELEVEN O'CLOCK was a long time coming.

After Seth and Sarah had gone on their way, and Sadie had paid the backyard one last visit,

Shauna locked up the house, set the security grid and headed up the stairs to bed. Tired as she was, her achy body protested the thought of just lying down and waking up stiff and sore. So she put on a Josh Groban CD, turned on the hot water and poured bubbles and spearmint oil in the tub so she could have a good soak.

She had plenty of good reasons to pamper herself. Her son was going undercover on an open-ended assignment. That meant something deep, something long-term, something dangerous—more than enough to give a mother nightmares. Yours Truly had sent her another threat. Eli Masterson had discovered those threats. His disregard for the chain of command was getting under her skin. Eli Masterson was getting under her skin, period. Each touch, each verbal sparring match, kindled something closer to desire than annoyance.

With the minty steam filling her nose and taking the edge off her anxiety, Shauna stripped off her silk robe ánd stepped into the luxurious bath. Her ouchy knees protested as she sank in up to her shoulders, but then the warmth gradually began to soothe the scrapes and bruises, and Shauna gave herself permission to close her eyes and relax.

Her day couldn't get any worse.

She almost laughed when the phone rang.

Served her right for dropping her guard, for pretending the stress could go away.

By the third ring, she was done debating whether or not to let it go to the machine. If it was Eli or Michael Garner, they'd only show up in person if she didn't answer. Shauna climbed out into the cold shock of air as bubbles and water slicked off her steamy skin. If it was Seth... No, she wouldn't go there. Besides, he hadn't been gone long enough to get himself into trouble. She hoped. Bypassing the towel, she pulled on her robe and hurried into the bedroom.

And if it was *him*...

Shauna paused and stared at the caller ID. *Out of area.* The wet silk was sticky on her skin as she tugged it together at her neck and tried to ward off a sudden chill.

No way. Yours Truly clung to the anonymity of a piece of paper. He lived in the shadows of her world, neither seen nor heard. He wouldn't have the guts to call.

With that thought wavering inside her head, she picked up the phone beside her bed. "Commissioner Cartwright."

"Shauna, sweetheart."

Faulty deduction. Her day *could* get worse.

She should have ducked under the bubbles and let the dog answer.

"Austin. It's late."

"I know, babe." Her ex-husband sounded pleased that she could still recognize the sound of his voice. "But this is too important. I need to see you. Tonight."

Chapter Five

Shauna couldn't believe she was standing at her front door in her nightgown and robe, hanging on to the dog so she wouldn't bolt out into the night, having this discussion with her ex-husband. "I asked you not to come over."

Sadie lurched in her grip, anxious to sniff their uninvited guest. While Shauna pulled her back and gave the command to sit, Austin somehow managed to work his way closer to the threshold.

"You said to call your office tomorrow and you'd check your calendar." Austin chose *now* to get the details right? "Look, honey, this deal can't wait. If I don't pony up in the next forty-eight hours, the opportunity will be gone."

If she wouldn't have had to open the door a second time to let Sadie back inside, Shauna would have released the hound to drive Austin back with a tail-wagging welcome while she locked the storm door. If she'd been thinking straight, she wouldn't have opened the outside door in the first place.

But after Seth's earlier announcement, and with her ex's connections to the gambling world, she'd thought Austin's midnight knock and claim that this was an "emergency" meant something horrible had happened already. Maybe Austin had heard or done something which could jeopardize Seth's cover. Though she'd long ago given up on the idea of loving Austin Cartwright, she'd never given up the belief that he wanted to be a good father. That he *would* come through if Seth or Sarah ever really needed him.

But, as usual, this visit was all about Austin.

"Number one," she started, enunciating every word so he couldn't misunderstand, "I am not your *honey* anymore. And number two, we agreed that unless it had something to do with Seth or Sarah, you and I were only going to speak through our lawyers. I'm not trying to be rude, but we have our own lives now. And mine includes getting a few hours sleep tonight."

"Give me ten minutes."

"It's never just ten minutes with you. Goodnight." Releasing her double-grip on Sadie's collar, Shauna pulled at the storm-door handle.

But Austin clapped his big, boxer-like hand against the door and wedged himself into the opening. Shauna groaned as he tugged her off-balance. If Sadie hadn't been there to block her fall, she would have run into his stocky chest instead.

"Austin!" The dog woofed to punctuate her mistress's frustration.

Never a big fan of pets, even a friendly pooch like Sadie, Austin retreated back to the porch, though his grip kept her from slamming the door. His craggy face, an aged version of Seth's, was wreathed with the boyish grin she'd once found so endearing. Now she understood it was meant to distract or placate. "This *does* affect the kids. I know I did wrong by them. I've been trying to regain their respect for years. This could do it. You front me the money and within a year—six months if I work my ass off, and I will—I promise to pay back everything I owe you. Everything."

"I'm not giving you any money."

"Who's talking about giving? I'm asking for a loan. To cosign at the bank for me. Once the casino's up and running, I'll pay back what I took from the kids' college fund. I'll pay it straight to them. They can use it for their kids."

Casino? Sincere as those blue eyes were,

Shauna had learned the hard way not to put her faith in his best-laid plans. Austin's heart might be in the right place, but his judgment and reliability had been altered by his addiction. Digging her fingers into the soft fur beneath Sadie's collar, Shauna grounded herself. She'd given him too many second chances already. She wouldn't be swayed by the hope in his eyes or her own wishful what-if's. "When was the last time you went to a GA meeting?"

Austin's smile evaporated. "This isn't a gamble. It's an investment. I just need a stake so I can get in on the ground floor."

"A stake?" Sadie barked again, picking up on the rising tension. "Do you hear yourself?"

"Could you shut Fido up there? I'm trying to have a conversation."

Sadie's bark deepened at his terse impatience. Great. Shauna pulled her back. "She'll wake the neighbors. You have to go."

Since he wouldn't let her close the storm door, she'd shut him out by locking the interior latch. But Austin's foot and a ready apology were there, preventing escape without him following her into the house. "I'm sorry, honey. Bad choice of words. When I mentioned a new casino, I was talking about working the business end of it—not making a wager at the blackjack table."

"You're an architect, Austin. At least, you used to be. What do you know about running a business?"

"I'm not betting on a Chiefs game!" He pounded his fist against the door frame. Sadie woofed. A growl vibrated beneath Shauna's fingers.

"Go now, Austin."

"Damn dog." Sweat had popped out on his top lip, even though the night was cool. "I'm talking about becoming a partner. About owning something again. This could turn into a real job for me. A new career."

Like he needed to be working anywhere near temptation.

"I hope it works out for you. But—"

"Is there a problem, boss?" Eli's deep voice came from the shadows at the bottom of the steps.

Hadn't she sent him home? Didn't anybody listen to her anymore? But instead of taking offense, Shauna trembled with a relief she didn't know she needed to feel. "Detective Masterson."

As Eli climbed the steps, Austin spun around, assuming a proprietary role she hadn't asked him to. "You know this guy?"

Those dark gold eyes were unreadable as Eli moved into the circle of light cast by the porch lamp. "She knows me."

His tie was gone, his collar unbuttoned. The plain white T-shirt exposed at the open neckline contrasted with the beard stubble that shaded the long column of his throat. A sensation that had nothing to do with relief flip-flopped in the pit of her stomach.

"He works for me." She eked the explanation through suddenly parched lips.

Austin's shoulders puffed up as he faced off against Eli's superior height. "Office hours are over. It's kind of late to be paying a visit, isn't it, pal?"

"Funny. I was thinking the same thing."

"I'm her husband. If she doesn't have time for me, then she doesn't have time for you. Now move along, pal, and let her get her sleep."

Husband? A lifetime ago, Shauna would have given anything to have Austin looking out for her like this. But he wasn't earning any points tonight. She'd done enough negotiating today—addressing every problem, defusing every tension and keeping everybody as happy as humanly possible. But she was done playing nice. Her sore body, fractured patience—and eager dog—helped her make a selfish decision.

"*I'll* decide who I have time for," Shauna announced.

Sadie's tail thumped against her bare foot,

transmitting her excitement. Shauna intended to make Eli feel just as welcome as Sadie wanted to.

She let go of the dog's collar and Sadie charged outside, knocking Austin off balance. When he released the door, Shauna grabbed Eli's arm and pulled him into the foyer with her. Sadie, who had already given her loyalty to her stick-throwing buddy, circled around and scurried after Eli. She loped down the hallway toward the kitchen and begged him to give chase.

With the storm door now locked between them, Shauna looked through the glass at Austin's stunned expression. "You stopped being my husband about two years before we got divorced. If you want to talk business, you call me during business hours and make an appointment."

"C'mon, honey, let me in. It'll be the last favor I ever ask."

"Stop with the *honeys* already. It's too late."

"Sadie, sit." The noise behind her quieted at Eli's command.

Austin was still working an angle. "Lunch tomorrow, then. My treat."

"I mean it's too late for us. For this kind of relationship. I can't be your safety net anymore."

"I'm doing it for the kids, Shauna. Help me become the father they deserve."

"She's done talking, *pal.*"

The air behind Shauna warmed an instant before Eli's hands closed over her shoulders. His heat quickly seeped through silk and skin, and the subtle pressure of his fingers massaged the coils of tension that had knotted there. She locked her knees to hold herself straight when all she wanted to do was lean back into that healing touch.

"So that's how it is, huh?" Austin's gaze darted from Eli's possessive grip to the taboo emotions that must be written across her face. "You finally found a guy to put up with your hours? To put up with all your rules?" His eyes raked her from head to toe in a mixture of regret and contempt. "You give him what you stopped giving me?"

Her money? Her body? Her unfailing support?

Eli's fingers tightened with almost painful intensity at the crude words. He dipped his mouth to her ear. "I can make him go away," he whispered, curling a ribbon of moist heat along the side of her neck. "Your call."

Yes, it was.

"Goodnight, Austin." Shauna shut the door. She twisted the deadbolt into place, wishing she could set aside the pain and guilt just as easily. "Damn him."

Though she knew it was the desperation of

his failed life talking, the words still hurt. She'd given Austin all she had, until there was nothing left to give. Until walking away was the only way she and her children could survive. Knowing he could barge into her world and still make her feel as though she hadn't been patient enough, hadn't fought hard enough—hadn't loved enough—rekindled old doubts she thought she'd laid to rest.

"Hey." The pressure of Eli's hands altered slightly, reminding Shauna that he still held her. She leaned against the door, but was too tired to shrug him off. His palms skidded over her shoulders and rubbed up and down her arms. "Your skin's like ice," he murmured against her nape, teasing her with the insane notion that she could turn around and immerse herself in the warmth of his body. "You've got a reputation for being pretty cool in a crisis. But this is ridiculous."

She should have laughed. She should have ordered Eli to move away. She should have had the will to do it herself. But the friction he created between the silk and his hands released the minty essence of the bath oil that still clung to her skin. The soothing scent filled her nose and eased her fatigue. His soothing touch tended her battered ego.

"Shauna?"

Wrapped up in his surprisingly gentle care, Shauna could dig deep to find her own strength. There was more teasing than reprimand in her tone when she spoke. "I assume you've been parked outside somewhere, spying on my house?"

"Until you report those threats from Yours Truly, I—"

"Never mind." Shauna shrugged off his massage and stopped the rhetoric.

Eli's caring was an illusion. It had to be. He was just doing his job, trying to be the partner she'd asked him to be. He was a man of sarcasm and attitude and annoying persistence, not tenderness. And if he'd touched her again, right there, right then, she'd have ignored every last rule in the book and walked straight into his arms.

But he didn't touch her. Instead, he moved to the sheer curtains at the narrow window to the right side of the door and peeked outside. "Your husband hasn't left yet. You want me to go out and encourage him to be on his way?"

"It's ex-husband. And no."

Eli let the curtain slide back into place. "You invited me in. Am I supposed to be the boyfriend? Bodyguard?"

"Neither, Eli. Neither." Shauna hugged her

arms around her waist and joined him at the window. She glanced out at Austin, sitting in his car at the end of her driveway. "You think he can see us in here? Silhouetted against the light?"

"Probably. Why? Did you have some kind of charade in mind? I warn you, I'm a terrible actor."

She wasn't sure she could play a convincing femme fatale or damsel in distress herself. Shauna tipped her chin and looked up at the man beside her. His eyes were already studying her with curious interest. At this stage of her life, *boyfriend* was almost a foreign word to her. And a woman with her training and experience shouldn't need a bodyguard, right?

But some company sure would be nice.

Even a surly detective who pushed the limits of her authority.

"No games," she promised. Reaching up, Shauna brushed aside the strand of dark hair that fell across his forehead and let her fingertips linger near the bandage that marked the cut at his temple. "That needs to be changed."

"I can take care of it myself."

"Uh-huh. Just like I can do such a whiz-bang job of taking care of unwanted visitors at my door." An engine started outside, and the sound of tires spinning against asphalt screeched over Shauna's last nerve. She tucked her fingers into a fist and pulled away, cringing at Austin's noisy, but welcome departure. "Thanks for butting in, by the way."

Sadie pushed her way between them to prop her paws at the window and bark at the encroachment on her territory. Eli laughed and scruffed up the big Lab's coat, much to the dog's delight. "Yeah. Here's who should have been guarding the place. A little late, aren't you, girl?"

"She's a lover, not a fighter, that's for sure." The sense that she was bending some kind of rule by inviting Eli into her home eased as Shauna watched the two of them play. Maybe she could keep him around as a dog-sitter without violating any departmental protocol. "How long were you out there, waiting to rescue me?"

"Long enough." Probably since she'd dismissed him earlier.

"So you haven't had any dinner?"

A hint of cynicism returned to his smile when he switched his focus to her instead of the dog. "The head honcho can cook?"

She tightened the sash at her waist into a double knot and prepped for the challenge. "Better than you think. I'll fix you a sandwich."

Shauna headed down the hallway toward the kitchen and Eli trailed after her. "Hey, Sadie. Guess I'm staying."

The dog charged ahead to complete the parade.

"Just until I'm sure Austin doesn't get the idea he can come back and harass me about something I have no intention of being a part of. Then you're out of here, too. Understood?" She said it out loud for herself as much as for him. "After some food, you go home and sleep. Tomorrow, I need you fresh to run those interviews, not shadow me."

"Right, boss lady."

"And stop calling me that."

"Yes, ma'am."

"Eli..." It was hard to take offense at that irreverent baritone, though she knew she should call him on his cheeky idea of humor.

After pointing him to a seat at the table, Shauna returned to the front door to reactivate the alarm system and turn off the porch light. She was too busy thinking of an appropriate comeback to notice the man across the street in the shadows, watching her front-door drama with displeasure in his eyes.

ELI WASN'T SURE what he was still doing in Shauna's kitchen an hour later, though the two messages Austin Cartwright had left on her answering machine, asking whether that buttinsky detective was gone and could they please have a private conversation now, might have something to do with it.

In the meantime, Eli had no objections to eating the second half of her meatloaf sandwich. He'd already eaten a full plate of the best home-cooked meal—hell, the only home-cooked meal—he'd had in a week. She'd already snuck a half dozen bites to the dog lying underneath the table. If Shauna wasn't hungry, he didn't mind polishing off the delicious late-night food.

He had no problem listening to her share family stories about the framed children's artwork or cross-stitched tablecloth and napkins that adorned her kitchen. The funny misadventures and treasured hand-me-downs from another generation took him back to his own childhood—before the plane crash, before the drugs, before the disgrace of his partner's corruption. Reminiscing took him back to a time when he still believed in people, when he'd been able to trust an instinct as well as a fact.

And he certainly wouldn't complain about watching her work around the kitchen in those peach pajamas, either. Everything was covered nice and proper from neck to ankle, but even the faded gingham apron she tied on couldn't mask how the silky material draped and moved over her curves. The loose kimono sleeves reminded him of how toned the muscles of her arms and shoulders were—and how her responsive skin had heated beneath the touch of his hands.

She'd been wound up tighter than a cork about to pop. But stress wasn't the only thing she'd let go at the backlit window of her foyer. Something elemental, something sexual, had passed between them—a forbidden yearning that charged the air around them just as surely as the danger she refused to face.

Shauna might have invited him in to distract the dog and keep the ex at bay. She might have offered him the meal as a thank-you to put an end to the night. She might be doing the whole happy-homemaker bit to show him he had nothing to worry about in the Yours Truly department. But Eli had a devil working inside him and was in no hurry to leave. He was drawn like a moth to the warmth of her bright kitchen, and to the surprising fire of the woman pouring two mugs of decaf at the counter across the room.

"Cream, right?"

Oops. When she turned around and caught him staring, he should have looked away, should have made a joke or apologized. Instead, he boldly took note of how a blush deepened the pale green of her eyes, and how a wry smile gave the soft lines beside her mouth and eyes a beautiful twist.

"You'd better be lusting after the coffee, Detective, or I'll have to throw you out."

Eli grinned. A woman who had the guts to call him on it when he got out of line would definitely keep him on his toes in a relationship. If he did relationships.

As steadfastly as he avoided them, he was quickly learning that Shauna Cartwright was all about relationships. With her children. Her home. Her dog. The men and women who worked for her. With Kansas City itself.

The chemistry might be there between them, but it would be a volatile mix with an unhappy ending. Unstable and dangerous to them both. Shauna had no interest in the type of affair he could offer her.

Besides, the woman could fire his ass.

So while he indulged his wayward thoughts, Eli wisely minded his manners. "Cream would be fine, if you have it. Unless you've got a slice of pie to go with it?"

"Don't push your luck. Baking's a hobby of mine, but one I rarely have the time for." She set a steaming mug in front of Eli and sat across the table from him. "It seemed like I was fixing food around the clock when Seth was a teenager. But once he left for college and moved out of the house, I had to cut back on keeping all those goodies around with no one to eat them but me. The older I get, the harder it is to keep the pounds off."

Eli hadn't noticed any trouble spots. He buried his nose in the frothy, fragrant brew before his thoughts could form words and get him into trouble. While the aroma distracted him, the coffee needed a moment to cool off. So did he.

He supposed work was the best way to do it. "I know you want everything to be strictly business between us, but I have to ask about your ex."

Shauna glanced up from stirring sugar into her coffee. "He's not related to the investigation."

"He tried to back you into a corner tonight, and you told him no." Eli nodded toward the phone on the wall with the blinking red light indicating the two messages. "I take it this isn't the first time you haven't given him what he wanted?"

"Where are you going with this?"

"Maybe Yours Truly is Austin—or someone else with a personal beef against you. He could be using the Baby Jane Doe case as an excuse to make your life hell. It wouldn't be the first time a man stalked a woman, hoping she'd turn to him for comfort and protection."

"You think he wants the two of us to get back

together?" She cupped her mug between both hands and blew on it before taking a sip.

Eli turned his eyes from the thoughtful pout on her pink lips. He should have asked for an iced drink instead. But he was stuck with hot coffee and a slow simmer that was stirring things to life behind his zipper. *Smooth, Masterson.* He leaned back to put some more distance between them. "He could be using the threats to keep you off your game so that he can talk you into signing that loan he wants."

"Baby Jane's murder is definitely a case that pushes my buttons. He knows that crimes involving children are the hardest ones for me. An unsolved one eats at me until it's put to rest." As soon as she considered the idea, she discarded it. "But I can't see Austin planning that far ahead, staying with one thing for as long as those notes have been coming. And his problem is with money. He wouldn't have hurt that little girl."

Maybe the guy's timing sucked and the visit and calls tonight were motivated by weakness or greed, not vengeance. After what he'd seen at Shauna's door tonight, though, Eli wasn't quite ready to cross Austin Cartwright off his list of suspects. "We shouldn't automatically assume the killer is the person sending the threats. Anyone else have a personal gripe against you?"

"I'm sure a few criminals out there think I personify the establishment that sent them to jail. But no one in particular comes to mind." She laughed behind her mug. "Betty Mills."

"Your secretary?"

"Executive assistant," Shauna clarified. "I think she's always had a thing for Edward Brent, and resents that I took his place. Or maybe she just doesn't like answering to a woman."

"She did seem kind of old-school."

Shauna lowered her mug and propped her elbows on the table. "I can't believe she'd do anything disloyal to KCPD. Even if she does have a personal grudge, she's been a team player for thirty-five years. She wouldn't criticize how we handled a case."

"It's not like Yours Truly has made a public announcement."

"Betty didn't follow me to that parking garage."

Eli leaned forward and mirrored Shauna's position. "She has access to your office, your e-mail and your personal schedule."

"She wouldn't have misspelled the words in those notes."

"Unless she wanted to throw you off her trail."

Shauna retreated as though an invisible referee had rung a bell and separated them. "Enough of this. It's after one. Making-nice time is done. I handpicked you to dig into the Baby Jane Doe case, not *my* life." She grabbed both their mugs and dumped the coffee down the sink, sending a clear message that she was done talking. "You don't need to report to me again until you know something about her murder or the task force investigation."

Eli stood, nudging aside the dog that had been dozing beside his chair. "Yes, ma'am. But if I decide my investigation requires nosing around into Betty Mills's or your ex's or anyone else's background, I will. That's how I do my job."

The telephone rang, adding a jarring punctuation to his defiant claim.

He watched the jolt of being startled tighten Shauna's shoulders. "This is ridiculous." She stormed across the kitchen and eyed the offending appliance. "'Out of area' again." She snatched the receiver off its hook. "Dammit, Austin. Give it a rest. You can call me tomor—"

Everything in Shauna stilled.

Everything in Eli went on alert.

"Excuse me?" Her body came back to life on a deep, sharp breath. "Who is this?"

Eli circled the table so she could see him as he approached. "Let me talk to him," he whispered, knowing damn well who was on the other end of that line, but only able to imagine what vile threats were being uttered this time. "Shauna."

She warned him off with a shake of her head and punched a button on the answering machine. "I'm recording this conversation, you coward. If you have a problem with…" Her cheeks blanched a dangerous shade of pale. "Hello?"

Eli pried the phone from her grasp. "This is KCPD…"

Silence.

The bastard had nothing to say to him.

"How did he get this number? It's unlisted." With her arms hugged tight around her waist, Shauna backed away. "How the hell did he get my number?" Her face flushed with color. She paced off the length of the kitchen, with a worried Sadie trotting along in her wake. "He asked why I was entertaining men at my house tonight. He said I should be saving my strength for what's coming, that I wasn't as smart as he gave me credit for." Her footsteps stuttered, along with her breath. "He knows what I'm wearing."

While she peeled off her apron and threw it onto the counter, Eli punched the play button to hear the last words of a tinny, mechanically altered voice. "…don't get it, do you, Ms. Cartwright? You've had your last warning. I'm not playing anymore."

Eli wanted a black-and-white unit here. Now.

He hung up the phone, removed the tape and pulled his personal cell off his belt. He punched in a nine and a one before Shauna wheeled around on him and snapped the phone shut.

"No! You can't call anyone."

"Dammit, Shauna, he can't make a threat like that and get away with it."

Sometime in the past hour, he'd stopped thinking of her as the commissioner of police and had simply seen a woman being tortured for no good reason. A woman he cared about. There was no boss or chain of command that applied here. Eli had to protect her.

But the woman he wanted to protect was dashing down the hall. "He may still be out there."

"Whoa." Eli caught her in three long strides. "You're unarmed. Unprepared."

"Let go of me!" She twisted out of his grip. "I'm sick of him having the advantage. I want to see his face."

"Shauna." He reached for the back of her robe as she switched directions and headed up the carpeted stairs. To get her gun? To get some clothes? "Stay put and let me go out and check the block. Call in a cop you trust—your son— to do a drive-through of the neighborhood."

He couldn't hang on to the silk, either. "I can't call Seth."

"Why not? Because he has the sense to worry about your safety when you won't?"

She turned on him and marched back down the stairs. "That creep said…that you and I… oh, God, he was crude." She whipped her twisted robe from between her knees and spun around. "I need to get dressed."

Alarmed by her mistress's distress, Sadie bolted past Eli. Shauna stepped on a paw and stumbled as Sadie yelped. "Stupid dog! Get out of my way!"

That was not normal.

"Hey." Eli snugged an arm around her waist, easily absorbing the brunt of her fall. Sadie ducked for cover.

Shauna dug her fingers into his forearm and twisted against his hip. "Let go of me."

"I'm not the enemy here."

"Let go!" She kicked against the stairs to push him off balance. "I need to find him. I have to stop him."

"Hey!" Eli lifted Shauna off her feet and carried her away from the leverage of the stairs. He cinched his arms around her flailing body, squeezing her tightly until she stopped struggling.

Once he was fairly certain she wouldn't do

any harm to him or herself, Eli altered his grip and turned her in his arms.

"You're scaring the dog," he whispered into her ear.

Shauna laughed against his collar. Or maybe that hiccupping sound was the tightly controlled sound of a sob escaping. What Eli did understand was that her hands were sliding up between them, curling beneath his lapels as they sought something to hold on to.

"I'm sorry." Her lips tickled the base of his throat and the desire to do more than soothe and protect heated his blood. "Is Sadie okay? I didn't mean…"

"She's fine."

Eli shifted to accommodate their difference in heights. Ignoring the friction of Shauna's soft curves sliding along his harder frame, he widened his stance and lowered her onto her tiptoes. Curling his shoulders and arms around her, he found the flat of her back with one hand, the nip of her waist with the other. Then he buried his nose in the crown of her soft, short curls and held her, really held her, until her breathing returned to an even rhythm, until the feverish panic passed—until she wound her arms inside his jacket and held on to him.

"I'm sorry," she breathed against the middle

button of his shirt. Eli suspected that unnecessary apology was for him.

A warm, furry head pressed against his thigh and Eli reached down to pet the dog. "Mama's okay, girl."

"No, she's not." Shauna linked her hands behind his waist and snuggled closer. The dampness of tears warmed his skin through the front of his shirt. "I never fall apart like this." Sheer will could only get a person so far. And she was entitled. "I'm more tired than I thought, I guess. I'll be able to handle this logically and professionally once I get some sleep."

"I know you will." He rubbed soothing circles across her back, trying to ignore the other two things he felt perking through the front of his shirt. Double layers of silk and cotton left little to his imagination. Did she have any idea of just how thoroughly she could get his juices flowing? His attraction to her was completely wrong, and yet, holding her like this—being held—felt completely right.

Her fingertips stroked his spine above his belt, as if trying to placate him. But at her gentle touch, a deep, illicit longing surged inside him. God, he wanted to kiss her. He wanted to do other things, too. But he'd be content if he could just keep her in his arms throughout the night.

If he could touch her and know she was safe, know she was with him. He pressed his lips against her hair, taunting himself with what he couldn't have and shouldn't want.

"If you tell anyone that Shauna Cartwright is…"

What? Beautiful? Tough? Sexy? "Human?"

Her nod was a caress against his chest. "I'll put a reprimand in your file if you let that one slip."

Eli grinned. "Your secret's safe with me, boss lady."

"Thanks." He felt her posture tighten and knew the mood had changed. She pulled away, tucking her robe around her neck and crossing her arms as though hiding her body could make him forget the womanly shape he'd already memorized. "You're a good sport."

"A good sport?" He'd been thinking about getting in her pants, thinking about ways to make her break out in a sweat. Thinking about how he was going to survive the night on her couch or in his car, knowing she was sleeping upstairs in nothing more than that peachy, silky second skin. And all she had for him was a "good sport"?

"Yes. I keep everything locked inside pretty much. But when the emotions finally erupt… well, I'm sorry you had to bear the brunt of it tonight. I needed a minute to regroup. I'm grateful. But I can't lean on you like that. KCPD—Kansas City—needs to know I can stand on my own two feet." Damn, she was sincere. She was blowing off whatever had just passed between them. "I won't allow it to happen again."

"You can control it like that?" Sarcasm dripped from his tongue.

The tilt of one golden eyebrow showed that she knew he wasn't referring to the few tears she'd shed. "Goodnight, Eli."

"No way am I leaving you. Not with this kook on the loose."

"Please." She padded to the front door and typed in the code to release the alarm system. "Yours Truly has already seen you here. So has Austin. My kids have seen you. I think it's time to do a little damage control."

"You really want to be alone, with that guy out there somewhere, watching you all the time?" He regretted causing the shiver that rippled across her back, but she needed to understand that playing with her safety wasn't a debatable issue. "Shauna, I'm trying to look out for you. Especially since you seem bound and determined not to do it for yourself. I don't like the idea of you getting hurt."

"What you like or dislike isn't the issue." He saw the steel in her shoulders when she turned around and knew she was asserting the cop in her again. "We can't be feeling these things. It isn't right."

Their gazes locked, closing the distance between them without moving a muscle. "So why are we feeling them?"

"Stress? Proximity? Because we're both a couple of outcasts? Hell, Eli, I don't know. I've been divorced for ten years. I'm still no expert on dating. I can't tell when you're flirting and when you're really arguing with me. Yes, you ooze testosterone and I'm attracted to you, but it's just…hormones." She threw her hands in the air. "At my age, mine are all screwed up, anyway, so I'm not going to trust them."

"There's not a damn thing wrong with your age or how anything's holding up."

"Stop saying things like that." Though her cheeks dotted with color, she came back to link her arm through his and walk him to the door. Her pat on the back when she released him was as patronizing as the tone of her voice. "You work for me. We both work for the people of Kansas City. You probably feel a responsibility to me because I singled you out for an assignment. That's admirable, but it doesn't mean there's anything personal going on here."

"You think I'm naive?" Had she not paid attention to anything he'd said or done over the past few days? "You'll have to do better than that."

"We have to hold ourselves to high standards, Eli. I won't have anyone questioning my character or my ability to do my job."

"All right." He'd give her that excuse. He could put his libido on hold if he had to. But he wouldn't compromise on the job *he* had to do. "I'll do a walk around the house and the block. Then I'll be parked out front."

"I want you to go home and rest."

"Are you going to report that bastard?"

"Give me the tape. I'll keep it in case—"

Her excuses equaled a no. "I will be parked outside."

She tipped her chin for a fiery stare-down, but any protest died on her lips. "Fine. Do what you have to. But don't let playing hero get in the way of your investigation. Finding out the truth is the only kind of help I want from you."

"Yes, ma'am." Eli looked beyond her to the golden pile of fur curled up in the archway to the kitchen. "Guard the place, Sadie," he ordered, as if the dog understood. Then he reached for Shauna.

He slid his palm along her jaw and tunneled his fingers into the wisps of her hair. He angled her mouth up to his and covered her startled gasp with a kiss.

Another protest hummed in her throat. But when she braced her hands against his chest to push him away, she curled her fingers into his lapels and held on. Tugged him closer. Their noses bumped and the minty scent of her skin teased his senses. She stretched up onto her toes and Eli framed her face between both hands and deepened the kiss.

Her cool lips warmed beneath his exploration. The soft curves parted and he thrust his tongue inside to slide against hers. He tasted the heat that was her, and the coffee they'd shared. He knew there was a reason he had such a craving for the stuff. Now it would forever remind him of Shauna and this kiss.

That was it. Just hands and lips and tongues. But it was sweet, it was potent, it was perfect.

And it was time to get out while he still could.

Eli pulled away, relieved to see he wasn't the only one breathing a little unsteadily after that kiss. *Worried* that he wasn't the only one breathing a little unsteadily after that kiss.

"Making a point?" Shauna's husky taunt danced across every sensitized nerve in his body.

"Yeah." He reached for the door latch behind him, needing the cool air of the night, and the dangers hiding there, to purge the need from his body. "I'm glad you don't feel anything, either."

Chapter Six

"Call never happened. Kiss never happened." Shauna huffed the cleansing mantra in rhythm with every stride, letting the tension on Sadie's leash pull her an extra half mile on their morning run. "Last night went away. Shauna rules today." She inhaled deeply and buzzed her lips on the exhale. "Shauna rules today."

If she ran long enough, pushed hard enough, said the words often enough, she might start to believe that her world hadn't been tilted on its axis half a dozen times in the past few days. Maybe she couldn't control the events, but she could control her reaction to them.

Seth was a well-trained cop. He was smart and strong. He'd be just fine on his first deep-cover assignment. She had faith in KCPD. She had faith in her son.

Yours Truly might have her life under a microscope, but he couldn't see inside her head.

She wouldn't let him wear her down, wouldn't let him outthink her. She'd uncover his identity before she let him uncover her fears.

Baby Jane Doe's murder wasn't a make-or-break career case. Shauna wanted the right answer to every crime. The slaughtered little girl with no mother to love and miss her was just another victim who deserved justice. Like every other victim.

And Eli Masterson's kiss was just a kiss. A mixture of amped-up tension, an available man and transitioning hormones run amok.

She could control what she felt.

She pounded off the mantra beneath her Nikes. "Shauna's in control today."

Exhaustion should have carried her right to sleep last night after Eli left. Instead, she'd shivered beneath the covers, missing the heat he generated inside her each time they matched wits. She'd hugged one pillow, then two, missing the surrender of strength, and then the rebirth of it, she'd felt when Eli had held her. And then she'd kicked the bedspread aside, feeling scratchy and hot, her half-dozing mind anxious to recapture the sensation of being possessed. Powerful and vulnerable, all at the same time. From just a simple kiss.

Yeah, right. She had everything under control.

Well, at least no one else had to see how crazy things were inside her. Maybe *that* would be the one thing she could control.

She pulled her shoulders back and turned the corner toward home. The cell phone in her fanny pack chirped. "What now?"

Shauna slowed her stride, but didn't stop. She and the dog both needed a gradual cool-down before they ended their run. After the second chirp, she unzipped the bag and dug through the dog treats and water bottle inside to pull out her phone. A glance at the number had her looking over her shoulder and glaring at the driver of the black SUV that had followed them all the way to the park and back.

Damn, the man was persistent.

She pressed the Talk button and kept jogging. "Eli?"

"Good. You checked who it was before you answered." His deep voice was gravelly from a deficit of sleep, but the attitude was still there. "Unidentified callers go to your voice mail or the machine. You don't pick up."

"I'm running, Detective. Unless you found a hole in Donnell Gibbs's confession while you sat in your car last night, I don't have time for more security tips. I still have to clean up and get to work within the hour."

"Me, too. I thought we'd better lay some ground rules before we went our separate ways."

Separate? He was really going to leave her? Uncomfortably distracted by *that* reaction, she nearly tripped over Sadie's leash. Time to slow this run down to a walk.

The shade from the tall oaks lining the sidewalk cooled the sweat at the small of her back and around the strap of the visor she wore. "Ground rules for what? You do your job. I do mine." She swallowed hard, buying time to ease the breathiness from her voice. "If the entire city hasn't found out yet that you're working a special investigation for me, then we keep our connection secret until we have something tangible to report to the media. As far as I'm concerned, those are the only rules that matter."

The black vehicle rolled up beside her and matched her speed. Though she refused to acknowledge him when the neighbors—or someone else—might be watching, she knew he was looking out the passenger window at her. "Make a list of three people you trust. I want you to be with one of them at all times."

"I can't work that way."

"I don't want you to be alone. Don't give this guy an opportunity to take his threats to the next level."

Shauna laughed at the irony of his request. "I'm in meetings with cops all day. Isn't that safe enough for you?"

"What about lunch?"

"I'm meeting with Austin."

"No."

Shauna crossed in front of him when he stopped at the last intersection. She paused long enough to make eye contact. "You can't tell me no."

"Where are you meeting him?"

Even a windshield couldn't diffuse the intensity of those dark gold eyes. Ridiculous as it was to be having this conversation by phone when he sat only a few short feet away from her, Shauna was glad to have the technology to keep them apart.

Because his gaze washed over her like a tangible caress, reawakening every pore of her body to the memory of being held in his arms. The tips of her breasts tightened, her toes curled. Goose bumps pricked her skin despite the heat generated by her workout. Her lips tingled with the memory of his tender demands, and some unseen gravitational trick seemed to pull her toward him.

But Shauna was stronger than any fanciful need or clinical reaction. She forced herself to turn away from those eyes and move on. "I've been a cop a lot of years," she spoke into the phone. "I've been dealing with Austin longer than that. I know how to handle him. I need to hear him out and make sure he doesn't involve Seth or Sarah in his latest scheme. My answer will still be no, but it will be on my terms and not when he blindsides me in the middle of the night."

"Where's the meeting?"

She reached her driveway and unhooked Sadie's leash. "You have your own schedule to keep."

"Where, Shauna?"

"The Union Café. At the train station downtown. It's a very public place."

"I'll be there, too."

"You can't—"

"I'll be part of the public. You won't know I'm there."

How could she not sense his presence after exchanging such a heated look? Without turning around, she knew where he pulled up to the curb a few houses farther down the street. "I guess if anyone spots you, we could excuse it as a work-related encounter."

"*If* anyone spots me. I'll be more interested in watching the crowd than anyone else will be interested in me." He paused long enough for

Shauna to type in the security code at the front door and insert her key in the lock. But the conversation wasn't over. "When's your last meeting of the day?"

"Oh, no. You are not coming over to my house again. I don't want you sleeping in your car every night."

"Where would you like me to sleep?"

His wink-wink delivery gave her a shiver of anticipation which she quickly squelched by shooing the dog inside and shutting the door behind her. "At your home, Eli. In your bed."

"Really?"

"Alone," she clarified.

"Party pooper. Actually, I was thinking we need to set up some kind of code so I can alert you when I have something to report. Put me on your calendar for five o'clock. We'll make the arrangements, and then I'll follow you home."

"Do you even understand the word *no?*"

She knew she'd set herself up when she heard the grin coloring his voice. "You picked me for this job because I *don't* do what I'm told."

"If Shauna thinks KCPD can get me something, I'd love to hear it. Personally, I've argued stronger cases. And this one seems to be getting weaker by the moment."

Assistant District Attorney Dwight Powers reminded Eli of a commando in disguise. The suit and tie and hint of gray in his hair fitted the trappings of a lawyer, but there was a graceful ferocity to the way he took the stairs down to the interview rooms at the city jail. A calculating alertness in the way he signed his name and allowed the guard to scan him. A plain-speaking expectation in his tone that Eli could respect.

Despite the district attorney's office's official approval of the case handed to them by the task force, Eli was beginning to see that he and Shauna weren't the only two people in Kansas City not completely satisfied with the job that had been done. "How many times has Gibbs's trial been delayed?"

Dwight shrugged his big shoulders. "I'd have to check the file to tell you how many motions have been argued already—and how many defense attorneys Gibbs has gone through. But I can tell you, if this was a rock-solid case, Gibbs would be in prison already. I've got a confession that's shaky at best, his criminal record and some circumstantial evidence. I imagine we could convict him on sentiment alone, but that's not how I like to work."

Eli signed over his weapon and the guard scanned him. "You think a jury will ignore the facts and convict this guy just because the crime is so heinous?"

"If they do, they'll be setting the grounds for an appeal. If the judge doesn't rule a mistrial first." They waited for the gate to close behind them before the second one was opened. "Is there something Shauna's not telling me about KCPD's investigation? Some reason why Internal Affairs is involved?"

Eli followed Dwight through the sliding steel bars before answering. "It's not unusual on such a high-profile case for I.A. to follow up on any inconsistencies in the task force's investigation."

"Inconsistencies?"

"More like tying up loose ends," Eli amended. "KCPD is just as interested in making sure this case sticks as you are."

"Uh-huh." Dwight nodded to the guard, who opened a steel door and waved them both inside. When the door closed behind them, Dwight turned and leveled his stony gaze at Eli. "Is this guy gonna get off?"

"I'm conducting a routine investigation," Eli insisted.

"Don't give me that crap." Dwight moved half a step closer. "I prosecuted your partner, Joe Niederhaus, a few years back, Masterson. He had a bad habit of blackmailing cops into tampering with evidence and intimidating witnesses to get the bad guys off. Including the man who killed my first wife. I'm not going to have any surprises like that come back to bite me in the butt at trial, am I?"

Eli stood straight, not even batting an eye at the veiled accusation. He'd had a lot of practice deflecting the guilt-by-association charges over the years. Though the shot at his character rubbed salt in the old wound, Eli had learned to play it cool. "Look at it from my perspective. If your partner was doing time for messing up police investigations, wouldn't you be extra careful about dotting your *I*s and crossing your *T*s?" Eli could lean in and intimidate, too. "So that no one confuses your work with his?"

Dwight released a slow breath. He gave a curt nod, as though that answer satisfied him. For now. But the tension in the insulated room eased and Dwight took a seat at the table. "So tell me about these *inconsistencies.*"

The A.D.A. was sharp. He picked up on word choices and intonations the same way Shauna did. Might as well share what part of the truth he could. "The main thing I'd like an answer to is, who is Baby Jane Doe? We can put this man away for her murder, but I'd find a little more justice if he knew exactly whose life he was paying for. I'd like to give that girl's family some closure as well."

"You're looking for names?" A snicker shook Dwight's barrel chest. "Wait 'til you meet Gibbs. I'm surprised he can come up with his own, much less that little girl's."

Eli thought Dwight was referring to a suspect's reluctance to reveal anything that might incriminate himself. But after five minutes of watching the skinny little black man pace from wall to wall to wall around the interview room, while his latest court-appointed attorney kept urging him to sit still, Eli began to recognize the symptoms of a recovering addict.

It was more than the nicotine patch sticking out from under the sleeve of Gibbs's orange jumpsuit. It was more than the wild, spongy hair, twisted into haphazard peaks by nervous hands. It was the almost manic desperation of a man looking for a comfort zone that reality couldn't yet give him.

Donnell Gibbs might be clean, but it was recent, and it wasn't by choice. His attention was focused on himself and any trick he could use to cope. Whatever was left of his fried brain was hard-wired to get him from one minute to the next and nothing else. Forcing him to focus on events that had occurred two years in the past was like asking him to fly to the moon.

"Don't ask." Dwight leaned over toward Eli's chair. "We did a psych eval on him. Below normal intelligence, but not handicapped. He's fully aware of events surrounding Baby Jane's murder and disposal of the body, he hasn't recanted his statement to the police and he understands the difference between right and wrong and how he'd be punished."

"What did he use? Crack? Meth?"

Gibbs's young attorney tapped the table to get Eli's attention. "My client's past drug use isn't at issue. No current charges have been filed against him in that area. He's agreed to speak to you voluntarily today. I won't allow any new charges to be trumped up against him."

Dwight raised his hands to placate her. "Relax, Ms. Kline. We're not interested in any new charges. Detective Masterson's questions all pertain to your client's alleged involvement with the Jane Doe murder. Right?"

Eli nodded.

Appeased for the moment, Audrey Kline gave the go-ahead. "Donnell?" He angled his head toward her, but didn't face her. "We need you to have a seat."

"That's okay." Eli pushed to his feet and buttoned his jacket before approaching the tiny man counting dots on the acoustic paneling in the corner. "Donnell? I'm Eli. I'm a police officer."

"Donnell Gibbs." He stuck out his hand, but kept his focus on the wall. "Pleased to meet you, Eli, Mister Police Officer." Shaking hands was little more than a timid squeeze, revealing the faded bruises and scrapes of an old fight—not uncommon to find on an inmate accused of harming a child.

"You get hurt in the exercise yard?" Eli nodded toward Gibbs's neck and the strangulation marks still evident there.

"I live alone." Donnell quickly drew his hand back and started touching each dot with the tip of his finger. "Four hundred ninety-six, four hundred ninety-eight…"

Audrey Kline explained when Gibbs wouldn't. "He was attacked by another prisoner. My client is in solitary confinement now, for his own protection."

Eli hadn't expected this. He'd expected to find a hard, don't-give-a-damn lech who could hurt an innocent toddler. Someone with the calm foresight to cover up his crime in a thorough, unspeakable way. He'd expected to look into the eyes of a man who could kill if it suited his purpose—not the vacuous, darting orbs of a man who was lost inside his head.

Eli had seen that same absent look on a younger, prettier face. To think that Jillian could wind up like this—living in a cell, used up, battered, alone—attacked Eli's soul and left him feeling as if he was sweating from the outside in.

He'd anticipated the kind of flak Dwight Powers had already thrown at him. He could slough off suspicions and resentment and still do his job. But he hadn't anticipated this personal punch in the gut.

He had to remind himself that he'd gotten Jillian the help she needed, even if he'd been forced to play the bullying big brother to get her away from trouble and into rehab. Besides, he'd promised Shauna that he would do this. And since he wasn't about to let her deal with the animosity and danger of stirring up this mess on her own, he would get the job done right.

"You missed a number." Donnell's head tilted to the side at Eli's observation, though he never looked away from the wall. "Four ninety-seven," Eli pointed out. "You skipped it."

Donnell made some calculation in his head and moved his finger back to a precise dot. "Four hundred ninety-seven..."

"Did you kill a little black girl and leave her in the city dump?"

"Detective—"

Dwight shushed the defense attorney. "His confession is already public record."

Donnell answered questions between dots. "I used hedge-clippers so the police couldn't find out who she was. Too little for fingerprints or dental records. No one would see her face. Five hundred…"

"Where did you pick up the girl?"

"In the park."

Eli trailed him around the room as he counted. "What park?"

"Swope Park. In the sandbox."

"Did you see the girl there more than once? Did you watch for when she'd come to play again? How many days did you watch her?"

"Six hundred twenty-two…"

Not the answer to his question. "What was the girl's name?"

Donnell shook his head. "…six hundred thirty. Just a little girl. Pretty brown eyes. Pretty dress. Not as pretty as Daisy's."

Eli glanced over his shoulder and mouthed the question. "Daisy?"

Dwight pulled the information from the file in front of him and read it. "Daisy Watts. Six years old. Gibbs was convicted of molesting her in 2002."

"He served his time," Audrey insisted on adding. "He was released on probation into a halfway-house program."

Eli returned his focus to Gibbs, who'd moved on to the next tile and was still counting. "Did you assault Daisy?"

"It was wrong. I shouldn't hurt little girls." Gibbs touched the next dot. "Six hundred thirty-one."

"Did you assault the little girl with the pretty brown eyes?"

"I killed her."

"How?"

"Six hundred thirty-five…"

"Did the little girl's mother bring her to the park?" No answer. "Her father?" Nothing. "Did they walk or drive to the park?"

"Six hundred…" Donnell paused, thinking. "She was in the sandbox. Six…"

"What did the mother call her little girl?"

"Six hundred thirty-eight…"

"Did anyone say the mother's name? What did *she* look like?"

"Masterson." Dwight was getting impatient. "This is getting us nowhere."

Donnell's lawyer agreed. "The police and D.A.'s office have already asked these questions."

Eli put up a hand behind him to silence their

protests. He was beginning to see why Shauna believed there was more to this case than the story Gibbs had told the police. Her doubts were based on feminine intuition and a gut-deep instinct honed by all her years on the force.

But Eli had made a much more tangible observation. "Where's six hundred and two, Donnell?"

The black man tipped his head back and looked at Eli for the first time. For a moment, the blank eyes focused. Then he turned away, took a step back and pointed to a dot. "Six hundred and two."

"Where's two hundred?"

Gibbs went back to the opposite side of the door and put his finger on a different tile. "Two hundred, two hundred one..."

"Are we playing games now, Detective?" Kline asked.

Dwight Powers leaned forward with interest.

"Show me nine hundred, Donnell."

The black man shook his head. "Haven't got there yet."

Eli named two more numbers. Gibbs moved from dot to dot. He could tell Eli what he ate for dinner last night and the name of his first-grade teacher. He knew the Royals had won the '85 World Series.

"What did you call that little girl when you had her at your house? Baby? Sweetie? Honey?"

Gibbs hesitated. Eli watched his eyes move like a man searching for answers. "I took her from the sandbox."

"Why didn't you assault her? Didn't you like her?"

"Pretty brown eyes. Pretty dress."

"What was her mother's name?" Gibbs was getting agitated. "What was the little girl's name?"

Audrey Kline jumped to her feet in defense of her client. "He claims it was a random act. He doesn't know!"

Eli nodded. He let Donnell go back to counting and returned to the table. Random, hell. "He doesn't know."

Yours Truly just might be right in his claim about Gibbs's innocence. And if that was the case, then what else did YT already know about Baby Jane's murder? And how far would he go to make Shauna pay for the mistakes of KCPD's botched investigation?

Later, as Eli was re-holstering his gun outside the security gates, Dwight Powers asked, "So, you want to explain to me what we accomplished back there? Besides giving my opponent grounds for an insanity plea for her client?"

"Donnell Gibbs isn't insane. But I do think you have the wrong man."

"You know I don't want to hear that. We're up for allocution and sentencing in a week. Is your gut telling you something?"

Forget his gut, other than the fact it was beginning to twist with worry about a tough-minded, but all-too-vulnerable blonde he knew. "It's the facts, Dwight."

"What facts?"

Eli checked his watch. He needed to get down to Union Station to keep an eye on Shauna and her lunch date. And make sure no one else was keeping an eye on her. "Gibbs's memory works just fine. Hell, he remembers every damn dot in that room. The details of his story never change. Not from the initial task force interviews, not today. He uses the same words. He never expands, never corrects himself. He should be able to tell us Jane Doe's name and more."

Instead of feeling victorious, the certainty of that statement left him uneasy. If Donnell Gibbs didn't know the details of the crime he'd allegedly committed, who did? Yours Truly? Someone else?

"It's like someone gave him a script about the murder to memorize. He knows every line, but he can't ad lib. He doesn't know anything beyond what's written on the page."

Point taken. Eli's suspicions could blow the prosecution's case. Gibbs could walk free. Maybe some vigilante would murder him under the excuse of protecting his or her child. The city would plunge into another panic.

But unlike his former partner, not every man put his own success above the truth. To Eli's surprise, Dwight fell into step beside him as he headed toward the lobby and the street outside. "So who gave him the script?"

Chapter Seven

Shauna scanned the vast expanse of Union Station from her seat on the open second floor of the Union Café. Where was Eli? Behind one of the wrought-iron galleries above her? Mingling with the tourists at the information kiosk? Watching her through the windows of the train museum or following the groups of school children beneath the giant clock that marked their way to the science center?

She was certain that she'd be able to sense his presence—just as certain as she'd been that he'd keep his promise to watch over her when she was away from KCPD headquarters and their built-in security. But nothing. No shiver of awareness. No tingle of anticipation at the thought of sitting in a public place while that mysterious, unspoken link connected them.

Either he was as good at blending in with the

tourists and locals as he'd claimed, or she was alone.

And though that meant she had no sense of Yours Truly in the building watching her, either, she felt a stab of disappointment.

Dangerous as it was to feel any sort of attachment to the man, Eli made her feel safe. He made her feel alive with his challenging words and potent stares. Knowing he was in a room, in a building—inside a sprawling complex like Union Station—with her took away the chill of isolation that she'd grown too accustomed to living with.

Of course, she wasn't truly alone. She sat across the table from her ex-husband. But Shauna was more attuned to her surroundings, trying to sense Eli—or *him*— than she was to Austin's animated sales pitch. Besides, she'd heard all the lines before.

"The Riverboat is going to be a great casino, Shauna." Austin had dressed in a business suit for his presentation today, pouring on the gentlemanly charm and boyish enthusiasm that she'd once been so attracted to. "Sure, when it's finished, it'll be smaller than those big chain casinos on the river. But this one captures the flavor of Kansas City—the history, the jazz—"

"The slot machines."

Austin's laugh seemed forced. Or maybe it was just her own interest in the sales pitch that had to be forced. He signaled the waiter to clear their plates and bring some coffee before continuing. "The Riverboat will contain every modern amenity that the larger gaming establishments have, but the ambiance will be warmer, friendlier. The players and guests will feel like they're stepping back in time when they walk onto that boat. They'll feel at home. It'll be great for business."

A familiar dread blossomed in the pit of her stomach, drawing her fully into the conversation. "Austin, for someone like you, I don't think feeling 'at home' in a place where you could lose so much money is a good thing."

Did he just roll his eyes? "Like I tried to tell you last night—I wouldn't be managing the games, or even working with them. They want me to oversee the redesign. We've purchased an old steel-hulled steamboat. They want my expertise to refit it to its original grandeur, and then design the new additions in the same plush retro style."

Interesting as the project seemed, as perfect as such a challenge would have been for the young architect she'd first married, Shauna couldn't see anything good coming of Austin's involvement now. She told him as much.

Austin held on to the edge of the table and bristled. "They've already hired me to do the prelim designs. I've worked with the engineers to bring the project up to code. But when the design work is done, I can make my association permanent if I invest as part of the management."

"Look, I think the remodeling is a wonderful opportunity for you to get back into the field you love." Shauna had no problem encouraging him to work. "But once the job is done, I think you should take your paycheck and move on to the next project."

"The port authority has already approved the location and construction permits, the gaming commission has given us a license. It'd be nice if we had the support of KCPD behind us, too. We're not even open for business yet and your people are already giving the lawyers grief over parking and traffic and our patron security plan."

It was Shauna's turn to bristle. "*My* people? You're looking for KCPD approval? I thought this was a personal request for cash. Or did these lawyers already promise you something if you capitalized on your relationship to me? And just who is *we*, anyway?"

"Damn, woman. I liked you better before you became a cop. At least you'd listen back then."

"And I liked you better before you put

yourself and the next big deal before your family." Shauna covered her cup when the waiter returned, and she asked for the bill. This meeting needed to be over. "Are you going to answer my questions?"

"All right, Commissioner." Austin twirled the title around his tongue as if he found it distasteful. "A foreign investor is putting up fifty-one percent of the front money. They're shopping around for local investors, but those of us already involved in the project get the first shot at ownership shares."

Foreign investor? As in out of country? Out of state? Out of county? Was that a code name for *illegal?* KCPD had long had its suspicions, if not concrete proof, about organized crime getting involved with the arrival and expansion of legalized gambling on the river. Thus far, with constant scrutiny, businesses on the waterfront had kept it clean. The unfortunate crimes associated with the casinos thus far had been isolated, random events. Hadn't they?

"Even Seth thinks the Riverboat is a good deal."

Seth. Undercover at the casinos. Shauna tensed, switching from cop back to mom in a heartbeat. "You asked him for money?"

"I got a look at the new hires. He'll be working as a bouncer in one of the bars there.

I guess the city doesn't pay him enough, so he's moonlighting."

Was that what Seth was working on? Investigating a new lead? Starting an on-site observation unit? Forgetting her aversion to his tactics, Shauna reached across the table and grabbed Austin's hand. "Did you tell anyone at the Riverboat that Seth is a cop?"

"He told them, honey. Relax. I imagine they think his background will make him pretty effective at keeping the peace there." Austin turned his hand to squeeze hers. "Hey, if I had a reason to be there full-time after the casino opens, I could keep an eye on him. Make sure he stays out of trouble. Maybe reconnect with my son and become friends again."

You selfish son of a bitch.

No matter what she'd learned about an addiction like gambling being an illness, she couldn't dredge up any sympathy for a man who would use his own son as a bargaining chip to get what he wanted. Shauna set her money on the table and got up. "Austin—gambling destroyed my life once. And in case you've forgotten, it destroyed yours, too. So forgive me if I withhold my money and the blessing of KCPD."

"Shauna…" Austin stood and tried to give her money back. "I said lunch was on me." He glared at the curious couple at the next table. "What are you lookin' at?" They turned their eyes back to their food and Austin turned his frustration on her. "Sit down and let's finish this conversation."

"The conversation *is* finished. *We* are finished. Don't ask me for this kind of help again."

"Shauna, c'mon."

She ignored the pleading, the outstretched hand, the crude curse, and wove her way through the tables toward the circular stairs that led down to the station's main floor.

But she hesitated at the top of the stairs as a shadow of unease rippled down her spine. This chill was different from her anger at Austin, or her fear for Seth—and it was getting to be far too familiar.

He was here. Watching.

"Where are you?" She mouthed the words on a hiss of breath.

Turning around, she made no effort to hide her scan of every table. She even looked at Austin, sulking in his chair, absorbed in a conversation on his cell now. Everyone she could see seemed to have a purpose. But he was here. Her snippy confrontation with Austin had caught his attention.

A man wearing mirrored sunglasses entered

the station through the brass doors below her and Shauna recoiled. Had Richard Powell been released from his armed guard at the hospital? Of course, not. This guy didn't even have a limp. The man peeled off his sunglasses and greeted a young woman. Hand in hand, they headed for the fast food court at the east end of the station.

Not Powell. No gun. No threat. But the feeling was still there.

I'm coming for you.

Shauna clutched the railing behind her in a white-knuckled grip as the memory of a robot-like voice replayed last night's warning inside her head. *Save your strength, Ms. Cartwright. If not for tomorrow, then the next day. Or the day after that. I'm coming for you. Justice…will be served.*

The air congealed in her lungs. She forced herself to exhale, then breathe again. She would not let him get to her like this.

"Show your face, you coward."

"Ma'am?" The middle-aged black man who'd been their waiter touched her arm and Shauna jumped like a rocket. He quickly pulled his hand away. "Sorry to startle you. Are you all right? Was there a problem with your lunch?"

"No." No problem but the company. Pressing a hand over her racing heart, Shauna summoned a smile and apologized. "Everything was fine, thank you. I left a tip on the table—if my ex hasn't already pocketed it."

"Thank you, ma'am. Have a good day." He smiled and jogged down the stairs ahead of her.

Her smile crooked with genuine wry amusement. The waiter must be independently wealthy and didn't need the three bucks she'd left him. Maybe he just wanted to keep his distance from mentally unhinged customers who argued in public and cowered on the stairs. Or maybe, like her, the man had work to do.

"Get it together, Shauna." Steeling herself against the invisible enemy, she raised her chin and descended the stairs.

Her job was to coordinate investigations, communicate with the public and facilitate the needs of her officers and staff. She wanted to find out just what the vice squad or Mitch Taylor and his detectives suspected was going on at the Riverboat casino—and what role her son was playing in their investigation.

And that was just this afternoon's to-do list.

She didn't have the luxury of giving in to the paranoia that followed her like her own shadow.

Hey, boss lady.

A set of eyes, distinctly warm and more

forward than they should be, snagged Shauna's attention at the base of the restaurant stairs.

Breathing an embarrassing sigh of relief, she nearly stumbled to a halt as she spotted Eli at a table near the restaurant's entrance gate. Or rather, she realized that he'd already spotted her. The familiar dark head, with that spike of hair out of place on his forehead, was bent toward the newspaper he pretended to read.

All the bustle of the open-air restaurant, all the voices and laughter, footsteps and music, echoing through the cavernous station shrank down to the intensity of that golden gaze locked onto hers.

Eli was here. Maybe he'd been here the entire time. The knowledge that he'd kept his promise after all was a foolish, heady thing. Her pulse leaped, her breath caught. Her heart flip-flopped with a crazy mix of relief and anticipation.

The world flashed by in a blur and she forced her legs to move forward. She couldn't go to him in public, couldn't join him at his table or take his hand or throw herself into his arms. The commissioner couldn't beg a man who worked for her to kiss her again—couldn't command him to make her feel safe, feel sexy—make her feel…period.

And yet, in the milliseconds that their eyes met, a dozen silent messages were exchanged.

Questions were asked and answered. Support was given. There was a tease, a reprimand. And finally, there was a longing, an awareness that passed between them that neither space nor time could measure.

Did you find something?

Yes. Tell you later. Are you all right?

He's here.

He won't get to you. I've got your back.

You can't follow me.

Try to stop me.

Eli...

I've got your back.

Resisting the urge to look over her shoulder to maintain that precious visual contact, Shauna hurried past Eli's table. Her heels clicked on the marble floor as she crossed the station to the escalator that would take her down to the parking lot behind Union Station.

Twin bullets of heat seared her backside, diffusing the lingering chill of Yours Truly's malevolent gaze, and, even without turning around, she knew that Eli was following her. Hmm. Shauna dipped her chin and smiled to herself at her body's physical reaction to mental impulses. Was it possible to blush back there? Wasn't she too old to be feeling this naughty, girlish delight at a man's interest in her?

Or was she just plain crazy to think Eli's diehard need to protect meant something more personal charged the air between them?

Yes, yes and yes. As a mature woman—a woman with a badge—she would be wiser to concentrate more on protecting herself than developing any kind of dependency on her self-appointed guardian.

With her purse clutched firmly at her side, Shauna paused at the top of the escalator, scanning the people around her before walking onto the next moving step. Even with Eli around to provide backup, she didn't want to be caught on the defensive by Austin or Yours Truly or anyone else in a place where escape would be difficult.

She rode down to the parking level, turned past a row of offices and headed for the exit. She skirted a line of students, fidgeting for their chaperone's lecture on manners to end and their fun at Science City to begin. She held open the door for a deliveryman and his rolling cart and crossed the circular drive where school buses were loading a group of students from the early tour.

"Commissioner Cartwright!" Shauna jerked at the unexpected call, then groaned, recognizing the woman's voice, knowing what those determined running footsteps behind her meant. Maybe if she just kept walking... "Commissioner!"

From the corner of her eye she saw Eli threading his way through the herd of fourth-graders to get to her. Shauna risked a glance and warned him back. This was an annoyance, not a threat that pursued her. She saw the shift of his weight—the urge to charge forward and take action warring with the wisdom of keeping his distance and maintaining protocol in public. He wasn't breaking the rules by being here, but closer contact could be misconstrued as—

"Commissioner!"

Shauna released a steadying breath and fixed a serene smile on her face as a willowy young woman with a thick brunette ponytail and a notepad in her hand ran up beside her.

"Are you following me today, Ms. Page?" Shauna asked, as the reporter slowed to match her pace.

Rebecca Page was ambitious and unafraid, a combination that always kept Shauna on her toes. "I called your office. Your secretary said you were having lunch at the station. I'm glad I caught you."

"Oh?" Shauna kept walking. She'd have to have a word with Betty about keeping private lunches private.

"I didn't want to wait for your weekly press conference to ask this. I think there's a big story about to break at KCPD, and I want the scoop."

If something big was about to break in the department, Shauna wanted to hear about it first. Maybe she was the one who should be fishing for answers from the press. "Everything's business as usual. I can't comment on any ongoing cases unless I clear it with the individual investigators. We don't want to give anything away to the wrong people, you know."

"What about to the people who need to hear the truth? The citizens of Kansas City who need certain knowledge to protect themselves?"

Certain knowledge?

Sidestepping a pair of moms and strollers as they circled the end of a line of parked cars, Shauna spotted Eli crossing between the vehicles up ahead. A glimpse of sky-blue farther down the row begged for recognition inside her. But Shauna had more immediate suspicions to contend with. "My people do an outstanding job protecting the people of Kansas City."

Rebecca scoffed as if she doubted that statement. "Why hasn't there been any detailed press release about the Cattlemen's Bank shooting? Is that because you were involved?"

Beneath the excited chatter of schoolchildren, the hum of a car engine cranked to life, and the glimmer of recognition tried to register a warning inside her head.

But the younger woman, tall and slender as a fashion model, blocked Shauna's path and forced her attention. She could take the wispy thing down to the pavement if she had to, but Shauna refrained from indulging the unprofessional urge. "We have the shooter, Richard Powell, in custody. He sustained an injury when he refused to cooperate with police, and he's currently under guard in a secure hospital facility. A judge and the attorneys have already arraigned him at the hospital. He'll be transferred to a jail cell as soon as he's physically able."

"And what about the new developments on the Baby Jane Doe case?"

Shauna almost flinched. The girl was good at the set-up-and-attack tactic to catch an interviewee off guard. But Shauna was better. Years of practice at hiding her emotions allowed her to present a calm, confident facade with only the hint of a curious frown. "What new developments?"

"You actually said that with a straight face." For a moment, Shauna reconsidered the takedown plan. "The word I have is that the task force who arrested Donnell Gibbs is now under investigation themselves. All of their personnel files were requested this morning. And the case file itself is in your hands now. So what's going on?"

"My, my—you have been busy." So had whoever it was at KCPD who'd leaked that information. "It's not unheard of for higher-ups to review a case as important as the Jane Doe murder. It's been such a concern to the community and to the members of KCPD that we want to make sure everything was done properly so that there are no surprises at the trial. It's routine procedure for a high-profile case like this one."

The car engine revved, showing off its souped-up horsepower. Absolute awareness slammed into Shauna with the speed of the car barreling toward them. Oh, God, no—not here!

She didn't even hear the reporter's follow-up question. "But to involve Internal Affairs? That speaks to suspected incompetence or cover—?"

"Rebecca—move!" Shauna shoved the woman between the cars and spun around.

Children. Moms. Strollers. Buses. In a split second, Shauna processed potential collateral damage—every individual, every location. The blue car picked up speed, rushing toward her and the crowded station entrance. A tidal wave of certain disaster was about to strike.

Already shouting, already running—thrusting her badge out before her—Shauna pulled out her gun and pointed it straight up to the sky. "Police! Get inside!" She fired two warning shots. "Inside, now! Move it! Move it! Move it!"

The screams and scatter of dozens of patrons, fleeing the gunfire before they understood the real danger, were only a momentary distraction to what she had to do. Changing direction abruptly, Shauna lost a shoe. But she ground her toes into the asphalt and charged toward the next lane of cars, praying the sadistic driver would alter course away from the loading zone, away from the parents and teachers and station employees scrambling to get the children to safety.

Her lungs burned. The horrible screech of brakes grated across her eardrums. The stench of rubber stung her nose.

"Shauna!"

The car slung around the corner and sideswiped one of the buses, crunching steel against steel. "No! Come get *me,* you son of a bitch!"

She shouldn't have turned around. She shouldn't have given the enemy that beat of time.

Crying children and panicked screams became background noise to the deadly cacophony of glass breaking and metal scraping clear down to the core as the driver floored the accelerator and forced the broken car back into pursuit. The afternoon glare off the windshield prevented her from seeing anything more than the silhouette of a man in dark clothes behind the wheel.

"Shauna!"

She had to run.

She lost the second shoe while lunging toward the parking lot's exit gate. She felt the heat rushing ahead of the car, imagined the whoosh of air pushing her off her feet.

A wall of brown smacked into her from the side. Steel arms whipped around her. Recognizing Eli by scent, Shauna held on as they flew into the air. The car rocketed past in a vortex of blue heat as they crashed to the pavement. Eli rolled, hitting the ground first, absorbing the brunt of the impact, skidding until a crushing thud stopped them at the curb.

An "oof" and a curse and a searing heat all registered in the instant before he tumbled her onto the sidewalk.

Had they been hit? Or had the force of Eli's tackle carried them this far? Dizzy from the fall, Shauna was slow to sort out answers. Eli rose to his knees with her gun and took a bead on the car as it crashed through the striped barrier gate.

"No, Eli, dammit!" Clarity returned and she pushed his gun hand down before he could take the shot. "I'm not the only target here!"

Then Eli saw them, too. Two terrified kids

and their tour guide huddled against the wall just ahead. Any stray shot or ricochet might have had deadly consequences. The bashed-up car sped off toward the highway to the west.

"Hell." His chest heaved in a monstrous release of tension. And then he was sinking onto the curb, letting his hand and the gun dangle between his knees, sucking in deep breaths as super-charged adrenaline worked its way through his system. But the deep gold eyes bored into hers. "You okay?"

Other than some new bruises to add to her colorful collection, she was fine. "My feet are a little tender," she admitted, prying the gun from his unresisting hands and tucking it into her waistband at the small of her back.

Confident he was in the moment with her now and could be reasoned with, she raised her head to the frightened trio against the wall. "It's okay now. Why don't you move on inside the building?" She smiled a reassurance to them, then turned to take stock of the rest of the scene. "It's all right." She nodded to a bus driver who seemed to have his panic under control. "You. Call 911. Tell the dispatcher Commissioner Cartwright needs assistance at this location. Request paramedics and crowd control."

"Yes, ma'am."

Eli's fingers feathered the hair back from her temple, drawing her attention back to him. "We've got matching bumps now."

His touch was tender, concerned, and she reached up to pull his hand away. He couldn't touch her like that. Not here. "Eli…" He winced. "Oh, my God."

Her fingers came away bloody as he pulled his left arm back to his stomach, cursing through clenched teeth. Her dinged-up hero had plenty to cuss about. His sleeve was shredded from shoulder to wrist, from jacket to skin, and blood seeped from the ugly wound.

"Hurts like a bitch," he muttered, flexing his fingers to ensure that nothing was broken. "The shock must be wearing off."

Shauna's own aches receded when he tried to stand. With firm hands, she pushed him back onto his butt. "Stay put."

"We need to get you out of here."

"I said to stay put." Eli's eyes flared with interest as Shauna shrugged out of her jacket and unbuttoned the blouse underneath. "Shauna, I—"

"Keep it in your pants, Detective." Even if she wasn't wearing a sensible bra and slip to cover herself, she would have stripped to get to the cotton blouse.

Cool air breezed across her skin a moment before he touched a fingertip to the prickle on her shoulder. "But you have goose—ow! Damn."

Shauna cinched the cotton around the worst part of his wound to staunch the bleeding. "You're hard on my wardrobe, Detective. The least you can do is cooperate with me." She used the sleeves to tie the blouse into place. "Sit here and take a minute to regroup. I need to take charge of this situation before we have a riot on our hands."

He grabbed her wrist with his good hand and pulled her back down. "No. You saw that maniac. We have to get you someplace safe."

"Maniac's gone. I'm in charge. You don't move. Are we clear, Detective?"

He glared. "You're not gonna get a 'yes ma'am' out of me."

"Eli—"

A bright light flashed beside them and Shauna blinked. Rebecca Page stood over them, clicking off picture after picture of the speeding car, the chaos and the two of them together on the curb.

Man, she hated reporters. Especially when they wore a cake-eating grin like Rebecca Page's.

"Business as usual, my ass."

Chapter Eight

Damn. The story was going to make the paper a lot sooner than Shauna had hoped. At least she'd convinced Rebecca Page not to run any of the personal photographs that would draw readers' attention to her role in this afternoon's events. A half-naked commissioner on the ground with one of her detectives · could be easily misconstrued by the public and the police force. That she'd actually been the intended victim could stir up enough panic to completely undermine her authority, giving the naysayers and I-told-you-soers plenty of ammunition to put her into some kind of protection program and keep her from doing her job.

Plus, the young reporter had promised to stick to the facts she'd actually witnessed. A crazy driver endangering the lives of school-children made headline enough. Shauna didn't intend to give Yours Truly or the Baby Jane

Doe case any publicity that could possibly drive her stalker and any evidence he could share underground.

Shauna rubbed her arms up and down the scratchy sleeves of her wool jacket and surveyed the quieting scene from one yellow crime scene strip to another. Two hours had passed since she'd buttoned her jacket over her slip and skirt, and taken control of the chaos.

She'd organized the adults present and gotten every kid accounted for. Fortunately, any injuries were minor, and those who needed a hug or a hand to hold were given the comfort they needed. She'd gotten the first traffic cops who'd arrived to cordon off the area and direct the frightened parents who'd come to pick up their children. She'd ended the press briefing as quickly as she could and deflected an attempted hug from a worried Austin. The ambulances were gone and the damaged bus had been towed away.

She had no sense of Yours Truly having her lined up in his sights anymore, and wondered if he'd injured himself in the crash. Or if the realization that he'd endangered the very children he claimed he wanted to protect had made him disappear. If this was his idea of punishment, then he'd just pissed off the wrong woman. If his intention had been to scare her into taking him seriously and force her to find the answers to Baby Jane's murder even more quickly, he'd succeeded.

Though not in the way he'd probably hoped. Shauna was scared, all right. Scared for the innocent lives this bastard was willing to sacrifice. Scared for these children. Scared for anyone who happened to be in the neighborhood each time he struck.

She was scared for Eli.

It wasn't hard to find the man who'd put his life on the line more than once to protect her. Though he'd kept his distance, Eli always seemed to be someplace nearby—close enough to exchange a glance if nothing more.

She spotted him now, straight and strong, sitting on the bumper of his Blazer, apart from the remaining circle of plainclothes detectives and uniformed officers, talking on his cell phone. His ruined jacket and her blouse had been pitched into the trash. His shirtsleeve had been cut off, and his wound had been packed with a gauze bandage that showed seepage at the elbow and triceps. She could see the purpling bruise that marred his sculpted cheekbone clear across the parking lot.

Shauna was weary and sore. She could head home to a hot bath right now and not one of those men would fault her for it. She could drive back to the office and chew Betty's hide for letting Rebecca Page know how to find her. She could get on the phone herself and start tracking her own leads on the sky-blue Buick that had terrorized her twice.

She walked toward Eli instead.

His wounds had been cleaned up by paramedics, but he'd staunchly refused to get into an ambulance. To Shauna's way of thinking, his raw skin needed to be debrided and checked by a full-fledged doctor. And she'd rest easier if he had something more than a shot of penicillin to combat the possibility of infection.

Her shoes pinched the abrasions on her feet, but Shauna held her shoulders back and tilted her chin at a confident angle as she approached the circle of men.

She addressed Mitch Taylor, the ranking officer in the group. "Thank you, Mitch. I know this isn't your regular job description anymore, but I appreciate your help coordinating the scene this afternoon."

The barrel-chested precinct captain shrugged off the gratitude. "It's Fourth Precinct territory, and my wife and son are scheduled to come to Science City with his first-grade class next week. Trust me, I want this place to be perfectly safe."

"I'm sure it will be." Shauna thanked the

others, then turned to Eli. He looked paler up close than he had from a distance, which alarmed her more than she cared to admit. "C'mon, Detective. You're with me."

Eli, who'd been watching the polite interchange with a curious indifference, ended his call. "Yes, Holly, I'll have him check that. Don't worry about me... I'll talk to you later. You, too, sis." He clipped the phone onto his belt and stood, cocking an eyebrow above the bruised, swollen cheek. "Am I going somewhere, boss—?"

Before Shauna could answer, Eli swayed into the SUV. What little color he had left drained from his face. "Eli?" Oh, no. When his knees buckled, she slipped beneath his good arm and braced her hands at either side of his waist. She felt herself falling as he sagged against her. "Mitch!"

The big man was there in an instant to take Eli's weight and ease him back to his seat. With his arm still draped across her shoulders, Shauna sat right beside him, steadying him until the dizziness passed.

"I don't need your help, Captain." When he could sit up straight again, Eli brushed off Mitch's assistance and took a couple of deep breaths. "I guess I lost a little blood."

"Not amusing, Detective." When he stood,

Shauna moved with him, clinging to the reassurance of healthy warmth she felt in the taut muscles beneath his shirt. She led him around to the passenger side where Mitch opened the door. "Get in," she ordered, though she couldn't tell if it was the grateful boss taking care of her own or the worried woman who'd come too close to losing someone she cared about speaking. "I'm driving you to the hospital."

"The paramedics said—"

"You ignored the paramedics' recommendation, but you will not ignore me. We're going to the hospital."

He braced his hands against the open door, refusing to budge. "I can drive myself."

"Don't be ridiculous. I'm not going to risk you passing out at the wheel when I'm perfectly capable of driving you."

"The commish said to get in." Mitch Taylor's booming voice backed up her.

"I'm not Fourth Precinct jurisdiction." Eli turned around, nailing Mitch with his coldest back-off glare over the top of Shauna's head. "This doesn't concern you, Taylor."

"Detective Masterson." Shauna's tone was clipped and concise. Her hands were much gentler at the flat of his stomach, silently begging him to lose the attitude.

He dropped his gaze to hers, understanding the message. *Play nice.*

Though nothing about his stance eased, Eli pulled the keys from his pocket and dropped them into her hand. "Would you mind driving me to the hospital, ma'am?"

Raising her own eyebrow at his sarcasm, Shauna waited for him to get in, then hurried around the hood to climb in behind the wheel. The seat was a mile away from the pedals. By the time she'd adjusted it so she could reach the accelerator and start the engine, a good deal of tension had filled the car.

She looked from Eli to Mitch, still standing at the open door. "You two know each other?" she asked.

Obviously, better than either of them wanted to. Mitch was the first to answer. "You've been asking a lot of questions about my task force the past few days, Masterson."

"And I haven't been getting many answers, have I?"

She'd known Eli would take the brunt of any investigation into the cops who'd arrested Donnell Gibbs, just as he'd taken the worst of that dive into the pavement this afternoon. He'd never complained about being odd man out, about assuming such an unpopular role in the department. Oh, he'd argued the wisdom of her plan, sure enough, but he'd never once complained.

That she'd put him in a situation that intensified the detachment he lived with every day ate at her conscience. If it was in her power to make his job any easier, she had to try. "Mitch—if you could help…I know you and your team worked hard to solve the Jane Doe case. But there are some problems with Donnell Gibbs's story that just don't add up to me."

"I'll put out a call to everyone on the task force and…*encourage*…their cooperation." Mitch's promise might not be a willing one, but she knew he was good for it.

"Thank you."

Mitch caught the door before Eli could shut it. "If one of my men did anything they shouldn't have on that investigation…"

He let the possibility hang in the air. Maybe not so unwilling, after all.

Eli glanced at Shauna first, then back at Mitch. His loyalty was clear. "You'll be the second to know."

"Fair enough." Mitch touched a finger to his brow in salute. "Ma'am." Then he closed the door and tapped the roof, giving Shauna the all-clear to pull out.

Hitting the start of rush-hour traffic, Shauna

cut across Main Street and zigzagged south through a less-traveled residential area toward St. Luke's Hospital.

"This isn't the way to your house or my apartment," Eli drawled.

"I meant what I said, Eli. I want you to see a doctor about that arm. Besides the risk of infection, you nearly fainted back at Union Station. From blood loss, probably. I know it's a blow to your ego to let those other men see you hurting, but I'm not going to allow any officer of mine to jeopardize his health just because his testosterone's kicking in."

"My testosterone's just fine, thank you."

"Uh-huh."

The man always had a point to make. "I'll agree to walk into that ER and let the doctors probe and stitch to their heart's content as long as you promise to walk in there with me and let them make sure that bump on your head isn't something serious."

"My head's just fine, thank you."

When the answering silence lasted from one tree-shaded block to the next, she glanced across the seat to make sure he was still with her. Eli had leaned back against the headrest and his eyes were closed. "Eli?"

She reached across the seat to check the temp

of his skin. The back of his hand was still warm. She slowed the car to take a closer look. He wasn't resting, he was frowning. Squeezing his eyes shut and grimacing against...what? Pain? Anger?

"Eli, talk to me." She pulled both hands back to the wheel and stepped on the gas.

"You're speeding, boss lady." But his eyes didn't open. He didn't smile.

Better to keep him talking so she knew he was conscious, and she could concentrate on dodging parked cars along the narrow side streets. "That sky-blue car was the same one that ran past me in the parking garage. Did you recognize it?"

"Yeah."

"Once, I could dismiss as an accident. But twice? I want that driver for reckless endangerment, no matter what else I can prove against him." They topped a hill and Shauna made the quick decision to turn onto a one-way street. "I asked Michael to run the license plate for me."

"Already done. I ran it last night. The owner's name is LaTrese Pittmon. Small-time punk. Hc's done jail time, probation and lots of community service. Mostly drug-related stuff." So Eli wasn't about to pass out, and she'd been fretting for nothing. The rat. "I didn't get a good enough look at the driver either time to tell if he fits Pittmon's description, though."

"All right, Mr. One-Step-Ahead-of-Me, what did you find out from Donnell Gibbs this morning?"

"It's not what he says, so much as what he doesn't say. He tells the same story every time. Same details, same words." She heard a gasp of sound as he breathed through clenched teeth.

"We're almost there," Shauna promised. "Hang on."

"I think someone fed Gibbs a list of facts, then paid him or blackmailed him or just talked him into taking the fall for that little girl's murder. Hell, Gibbs is simpleminded enough—maybe he's actually convinced himself he did kill her."

"I suspected as much." But to have someone else finally share her suspicions didn't please her as much as she'd expected. There were still too many unanswered questions. Still too many people getting hurt.

"Pull over."

The sharp command startled her. "Can you hang on? We're almost—"

"Pull over!"

Shauna slammed on the brakes and swung into the first turnoff she could find. "Are you hurt?" They crunched over gravel and leaves into an alley between two backyard fences. As Eli unbuckled his seat belt, she slipped the car into Park and unhooked her own belt. "What's wrong? This is all my fault. I never should have gotten you involved. What are you…?"

As soon as she set the brake, Eli grabbed her by the shoulders and dragged her across the seat. "I don't want to play at this anymore."

His lips covered hers, muffling any protest. He crushed her to his chest, stilling any struggle. He coaxed the seam of her lips to open and thrust his tongue inside to claim hers, blotting out the thought of being anywhere else but in his arms.

Lying at an awkward angle, sprawled across his thigh and chest, Shauna could do little with her hands besides find a fistful of shirt and hold on. But there was nothing stopping Eli from skimming his palm down her back and squeezing her bottom. Nothing to stop him from dragging that hand beneath the hem of her skirt and branding her skin with a palm-print of heat. Nothing to stop him from tunneling his fingers into her hair and angling her face this way, then that, testing how the kiss deepened with every subtle nuance of position.

"'Come and get me'?" He quoted her words against her mouth. "What the hell was that about?" His chest shook with the fear he must have felt as the car had hurtled toward her. Or perhaps it was anger at her for putting herself at risk. He slipped his fingers to the buttons of her jacket as he caught her bottom lip between his. "Are you trying to scare the crap out of me, boss lady?"

"Eli, I—"

He covered her mouth at the same time he cupped her breast through her bra and slip. Shauna moaned in helpless surrender, suspended on a coiling tightrope of desire that ran from the heady flavor of coffee on his tongue to the pearlized bud of her nipple straining into his palm to the pool of liquid fire gathering at the heart of her.

"And then I couldn't hold you?" He kissed a gentle reprimand, kissed an apology. "I'm not any good at playing my life by someone else's rules."

He spread her jacket open and tugged it off her shoulders. The straps of her slip and bra quickly followed, catching in the crooks of her elbows and giving his roving hands access to more skin, heating every cell with every needy touch. He skimmed her neck and shoulders with callused palms, dipped his fingers beneath the lacy neckline and teased the swells of each breast with his knuckles. He reached inside with his thumbs and flicked the nipples to stringent attention. And when she whimpered her pleasure, he framed her face between both hands and kissed her hard.

Something inside Shauna unfurled, awoke at Eli's fierce need. The brittle shell of self-preserving protocol shattered and freed her to respond to the potent stamp of his kiss. This was an affirmation of life, an outlet for emotions too intense to keep locked up inside. And Shauna wanted more.

She bent one knee up on the seat, giving herself the leverage to free her arms and wind them around Eli's neck. She rubbed her aching breasts against him as she pulled herself up to become an equal partner in this embrace. With a satisfied moan deep in his chest, Eli adjusted his position so that there was more tangling of legs, more friction between angles and curves, more room for lips to taste a salty neck or nibble an ear.

A lot of years had gone by since passion had last consumed her, and Shauna had forgotten the tactile thrill of tracing where warm skin met short hair. Of burying her fingers in the sexy muss of silky spikes. She'd forgotten the contrast of firm lips and prickly beard stubble against her cheek. The remarkable differences between a man's hard need and a woman's softer welcome.

She'd forgotten a few things, yes. But she'd never known this crazy, raging heat that consumed her from the inside out. This need to connect physically, mentally and emotionally with a man.

With Austin, she'd quickly learned to hold back, so that when he disappeared on a gambling binge for a few days, or plunged her into some new crisis of lost money and dangerous company, she wouldn't hurt as much. She wouldn't feel betrayed. She could survive as long as she stayed in control. She could protect herself and her children if she didn't want anything—or anyone—too much.

But with Eli Masterson, nothing had been predictable or controlled. And as doggedly as he protected her, she wasn't really…safe.

Shauna's fingers froze against Eli's scalp. She buried her face against his shoulder, breathing in the scents of musky skin and sterile antiseptic. It was no good. She needed some fresh air if she wanted to avoid how being this close to Eli scattered her thoughts and clouded the truth. This was not a relationship. Groping each other in the car, sticking their tongues down each other's throats, was purely lust, right? A physical reaction to stress, not a heart-to-heart testimony to anything deep or lasting or real.

She couldn't throw away a career or a life by allowing either one of them to forget that.

Misreading her subtle withdrawal as the chill of the evening air or the remembrance of fear, Eli altered his hold. He moved his hands to the relatively neutral territory of her back and rubbed slow, warming circles there as he tugged her clothes back into place.

"That man tried to kill you today." Eli's voice sounded raw against the crown of her hair and Shauna shivered with the need to erase the pain she heard. But she couldn't. "I had to stand aside and pretend that you getting hurt didn't matter to me."

"Eli…I don't matter." Taking care to avoid his injured arm, Shauna pushed herself up onto the seat beside him. She needed to see into those dark gold eyes and make him understand the truth they had to accept. "I can't matter."

"Bull—"

"We had a job to do today, Eli. I couldn't let Yours Truly hurt those people. And you wouldn't let him hurt me. I thank you for that." She brushed her fingers across the back of his hand where it rested on her thigh. Then she gently moved his hand to his own thigh and scooted back behind the steering wheel. "No matter what you claim, you'd make a great partner. I can always sense when you're around, looking out for me."

"A partner?" The ice in his tone was unmistakable.

"I'm not offering you a job. The commissioner works alone." She tried to make a joke, but she fumbled with the buttons of her jacket as she redressed herself, giving away the unsteady state of her nerves. Finally, she gave up and clutched the wheel until the worst of the crazy need still sparking through her system had abated. "I hate it that you got hurt, too. I hate that some outside force has power over our lives like that."

She turned on the seat to face him, fighting to ignore the heartbreaking reminder of his bravery staining the long white bandage on his arm. "But maybe if you hadn't been so focused on me, maybe if I hadn't been so distracted by Rebecca Page's questions, we would have seen that maniac sooner. Instead of scaring forty-seven children half to death and ripping your arm to shreds, we could have stopped him. Maybe we could have arrested LaTrese Pittmon or whoever was driving that car, and we'd be on our way to finding out exactly who Yours Truly is."

"If I hadn't been focused on you, you'd be dead."

The cold harsh fact hung in the air between them.

Shauna stared through the windshield, searching the long alleyway for a rational argument that wouldn't come.

Her lips felt bruised and feverish—thoroughly ravished in a way her ex-husband had had neither the time nor the inclination to do. Shauna closed her eyes and touched them, reliving for a moment the passion she'd felt in Eli's arms. "This is crazy. It goes against everything I've been taught for twenty-five years at this job. Everything that ten years of a doomed marriage taught me."

She looked over and saw that Mr. Cool was dealing with the aftershocks of that torrid kiss as well. His chest rose and fell in deep, steadying breaths, and he adjusted his position on the seat to ease the strain on his anatomy.

"We have to focus on the investigation, Eli." Shauna released the brake but didn't shift the car into gear. "Or we won't be able to get the job done. *I* won't be able to do my job with you…in my space all the time. I need you to help me keep some distance between us."

"I'm that irresistible, huh?"

Thank God he could still find some humor in this. Maybe they could just go back to trading barbs instead of those dangerous kisses. "You're a pain in the butt is what you are."

"My sisters say I have a terrible big-brother complex, always trying to rush in and fix things—trying to keep them safe. It's my responsibility. I'm the closest thing to a parent they have."

"They're lucky to have you."

He laughed. "Not really. I'm lousy at it. That's why one's in rehab, making terrible choices in men, and the other's a workaholic with no men at all in her life. We're quite the happy family."

Shauna didn't see anything funny in the guilty weight he carried on his shoulders. "I'm sorry to hear about your sister. I know how loving someone with an addiction can throw your whole life off-kilter. The addiction affects every family decision, every personal choice you make." He nodded his agreement. Sad as it was, maybe this was the common ground where she could finally get him to understand her need for order and distance between them. "Is that what makes you so protective of me? It's ironic for a man ten years younger than me to act like my big brother."

Eli turned and looked at her so hard that Shauna felt herself backing toward her side of the car. But she didn't get far. Eli palmed the back of her neck, leaned across the seat and kissed her hard and fast, with the same intensity that darkened his eyes when he pulled away.

"Trust me. These are not brotherly urges I'm having toward you." He sat back, trying to be good for her sake, she supposed. Or maybe trying to make her want what she shouldn't all the more. "Now drive, before I bleed through the upholstery."

Shauna buckled up and looked over her shoulder to back out of the alley. "Or someone sees us."

"Yeah. That, too."

"MY GOD, Shauna. I just heard." Michael Garner entered St. Luke's emergency room waiting area and strode across the lobby as if she was the one getting half her arm stitched up. "Are you all right?"

Shauna tossed aside the magazine she hadn't been reading and stood to greet him. But he swallowed her up in a hug before she could get a word out. He held her a fraction too close, held her a moment too long.

"Michael." When she gave him a gentle nudge,

he hugged her harder. Good grief! When would the man get a clue? The lunkhead rocked her back and forth, though she wasn't sure which of them he was trying to comfort. "Michael."

With a firmer push, he finally stepped back. But he cupped his hands at her elbows to maintain contact. "I had to hear about the incident at Union Station on the evening news. Why didn't you call me?"

Actually, she was surprised he hadn't heard about it through the police grapevine any sooner. But he wore a genuine frown and Shauna regretted her harsh thoughts. She patted his lapel, offering reassurance as well as apology as she pushed him even farther away. "Half the precinct turned out once they heard there were children involved in the drive-by. I swear we even had a couple of off-duty officers show up. Believe me, we didn't need any more chiefs trying to help."

Michael pulled her into a seat beside him. "I meant, why didn't you tell me that Yours Truly bastard tried to run you down?"

"What?" She hadn't leaked a word about the previous threats to Rebecca Page.

No one besides her and Eli knew that those threats had become explicitly personal.

"I've been at this job longer than you have,

Shauna. I can put two and two together." He took off his suit coat and draped it around her shoulders, wrapping her up in his unwanted personal protection. "Yours Truly was becoming bolder with each message he wrote to KCPD. First, it was just a complaint, like a lot of other people. Then he threatened to sue the department. When he began accusing your task force of incompetence, I knew it was just a matter of time before he targeted someone specifically. It's you, isn't it, Shauna? He tried to kill you today."

Michael's friendly concern had just taken a left turn toward creepy. She shrugged off his coat and stood. "How much do you know about Yours Truly?"

He rose and tried to cover her frayed jacket and low-cut décolletage again. "You showed me his messages to the department. We decided not to give this guy any of the publicity he wanted, so we buried them in the files. But a threat against KCPD is a threat against all of us. Maybe it's time to go public about this lunatic. Put everyone on alert so he can't be a danger to any of us. Especially you."

So he didn't know about the personal threats. He'd just made a calculated deduction. Shauna breathed a little easier, but not much. This time she carefully folded his jacket and handed it back to him. "Listen, Michael. We don't know that what happened today has anything to do with the Yours Truly complaints. Maybe the driver was some kook off his meds. Someone under the influence." The lies flowed smoothly off her tongue. "Maybe he was just a really bad driver."

"And it's just coincidence that you were the one he nearly killed?"

"There were dozens of people in that loading zone and parking lot. Any one of them could have been the target—if there was a single target."

"Don't dismiss my concerns, Shauna. You're too important to this department." Oh, God, he was going to touch her again. "You're too important to me."

Shauna slyly moved beyond his reach and began to pace. The nurse had said the work on Eli's arm would take about an hour to complete. It was nearly that now. She'd like to send Michael on his way before he took issue with *that* part of her life, too. "I was targeted during the Cattlemen's Bank shooting. You didn't seem to think that was personal."

"Didn't I? Who was one of the first cops on that scene? Who offered to run the press conference for you so you could get out of the spotlight for a few minutes to get cleaned up and catch your breath?"

She had to give him that one. "You."

"Me." With a shushing gesture from the ward clerk at the desk, Shauna allowed Michael to take her elbow and steer them back to a quiet corner of the waiting room. "You know, maybe if you stopped flitting around with that Eli Masterson…"

"Flitting?"

"Secret meetings. Sneaking off for lunch with him."

"I didn't have lunch with Eli."

"You were both at Union Station at the same time."

Did Betty broadcast her private agenda to anyone who asked? "I was having lunch with my ex-husband to discuss a bad investment. Not that that's any of your business. Eli…" Oops, she couldn't afford to give Michael any more fodder for his "flitting" imagination. "Detective Masterson was having lunch at another table."

"Well, it's a good thing Masterson was there to save the day." He shook his head as he looked down at her. Talked down to her. "He's bad news, Shauna. You know he was partnered with Joe Niederhaus, right? The I.A. cop who almost blew the Arnie Sanchez murder trial? The cop who got other cops killed while he lined his pockets with cash?"

Shauna hugged her arms across her stomach, stemming the frisson of anger that threatened to spill over into a real fight with her deputy. "Detective Masterson is not Joe Niederhaus. You can't judge a man by the people he's worked with."

"You don't see any other cops lining up to be his partner, do you? And now he's sticking his nose into the Baby Jane Doe case? At the eleventh hour when we've already got our man? Do you think the guy has a death wish? Maybe another cop was trying to run *him* down today, not you."

Forget diplomacy. "That's it, Michael. We are through discussing this."

"Hanging with Masterson will get you hurt."

"I am not hanging—"

"Dammit, Shauna, I didn't come here to pick a fight. I'm worried about you. I care about you." He caught her by the arm when she tried to walk away. He wisely retreated, holding his hands up in placating surrender. "Maybe you should take a few days off. Get out of town— out of the country, even—where you'll be safe and you can relax and regroup until this whole Yours Truly thing blows over."

She didn't for one minute think the escalating threats were going to "blow over" unless she uncovered the truth before Yours Truly could carry out his ultimate threat. But leave the country? "Sounds like you're trying to get rid of me."

"I'm trying to keep you safe. You know I can run things for you if you need me to."

"I like the way the boss lady runs things." Eli's deep voice resonated through the air behind her, sending a shiver of awareness across her skin.

"Well, look who's here. This conversation doesn't concern you, Detective." Shauna wanted to turn away from Michael's told-you-so gloat as much as she wanted to see that Eli was truly all right. But she barely had time to note the green hospital scrubs stretched tautly across his shoulders before Michael took another stab at her character. "Are you going to tell me that this is a coincidence, too? Shauna, it goes against every rule in the book to fraternize with—"

"Don't quote me the rules, Michael. One of my men was wounded saving my life." He had the stitches and bruises and bandage to prove it. "I don't think it's out of line to drive him to the hospital."

"But it is out of line to drive him home and give him a little TLC."

The urge to slap his smug face itched through her fingers. But she knew a better way to put him in his place. "You'd better hope you never get hurt, Michael. Because you won't be getting any TLC from me."

"Just remember. I warned you about him." The *him* Michael was referring to had walked right up behind her, close enough for her to feel the warmth from his body, close enough to worry that he'd defend her honor against Michael's slurs with the same zeal with which he'd defended her life. "I don't want to see you lose your career, and I don't want to see you get hurt."

She looked away from Michael's final pleading glance, but Eli never so much as blinked at the man-to-man standoff that lasted all of two seconds before Michael pulled on his jacket and left the hospital.

"That was pleasant," Eli drawled sarcastically.

"Bite me." Shauna went back to her chair to retrieve her purse and her copies of the paperwork the clerk had filed for them.

"Love to."

"Eli. You just heard what he could do to me if he can prove any impropriety between us."

"Forget it. You're not getting rid of me."

She didn't think so. "Could you at least keep a professional distance when we're out in public?"

"Unless another car tries to mow you down. Then I won't make any promises."

"Eli." Reprimanding this one was useless. But unlike Michael, he gave her her space when she asked him to. "I have one more stop I want to make before I drive you home. You can either wait here or tag along."

Five minutes later they were standing in the doorway of room 3036, staring at Richard Powell's empty, pristinely made, unoccupied bed.

"What do you mean, he was discharged?" The nurse's aide didn't deserve the snap in Shauna's voice, but it had already been too long a day. She had her phone out and was dialing the jail's main desk before she apologized and sent the girl on her way. "I left specific instructions to be notified when Powell was transferred to lockup."

A clear memory of those ice-gray eyes chilled her as she listened to the desk sergeant's woeful story about a transfer mix-up with a petty criminal who was now locked away in a solitary cell while Powell had been mistakenly released. Eli was already leading her to the stairwell, his ever-vigilant eyes scanning each doorway and corner before they walked past.

"The man killed two people!"

The desk sergeant cursed and apologized.

Then cursed again. "I'll get an APB out on him immediately. Put the department on full alert."

"Do that."

"Yes, ma'am. I'm sorry...I've been distracted by—"

Now wasn't the time to listen to personal excuses. "How long has Powell been gone?"

The sergeant checked her computer. "According to our records, he was released this morning."

In plenty of time to get behind the wheel of a sky-blue Buick and try to kill her again.

Chapter Nine

"Mom, the kitchen's clean already. Have a seat and relax. It's gorgeous outside tonight. Come see."

Shauna hung up the dish towel and left the kitchen to find her grown daughter propped on the back of the sofa beside the dog. Both rested their respective paws or elbows on the sill of the turret window and stared out into the night. "By 'gorgeous,' you're not referring to that black SUV parked out front again, are you?"

She'd already endured a bout of teasing over the "dark-haired hunk" sitting in the shadows away from the street lamp outside, keeping watch over the place. Sarah tucked her hair behind her ears and rolled her eyes one more time. "I don't understand why you make him sit out in the car all night. You let Sadie in the house."

"Sadie's family," Shauna reasoned. "And I invited Detective Masterson in for dinner."

"Yeah, with me sitting in the middle playing referee while you two tried not to flirt with each other."

How did she explain departmental protocol and tempting fate to a hopeless romantic like Sarah? Shauna sat on the edge of the sofa and stroked Sadie's fur. "I'm the top dog at KCPD. My character has to be above reproach—even more so because I'm a woman in a position of authority. It's not fair, but it's reality. I have to be someone my men can look up to and someone the public can identify with and trust."

"The public can't identify with a woman wanting to be with an attractive man?" Sarah touched her forehead and cheek, emulating the marks Eli now bore. "I think the bruises and bandages give him a more rugged look."

Much as it pained Shauna to see the wounds sustained on her behalf, they did provide an evocative contrast to the sophisticated intelligence in those incredible eyes. She shook off the image that came to mind far too easily. Aesthetics were beside the point. "Would you want any of your parents to think you had some kind of relationship—beyond the classroom—with one of your students?"

"Gross." Sarah scrunched her face into a dramatic frown, then smiled and winked as she tipped her head toward the window. "But Detective Masterson isn't any ten-year-old. He's a full-grown specimen of tall, dark and handsome. And he's got the hots for you."

"Please. I'm ten years older than he is. He's much more likely to be attracted to a pretty young woman like you."

After that close encounter in the SUV on the way to the hospital yesterday, Shauna had finally rationalized that it was just the proximity of working together and the stress of a few close calls that had allowed any sort of attraction to develop between her and Eli. She was lonely. He was lonely. Yesterday, they'd needed each other to survive. Toss them together and it was a volatile mix. But she was smart enough to be able to differentiate between hormones and necessity, and something truly meaningful.

She had to derail her daughter's—as well as her own—foolish hope that any kind of relationship with Eli could happen.

"He had his eye on you at dinner," Shauna suggested.

Sarah laughed. "To get me to pass him the shepherd's pie or the salad bowl. I swear, if he were staring any harder at your backside while you were fixing coffee at the counter, I was going to ask you two to get a room."

"That's ridiculous." Shauna wouldn't admit that she'd felt that appreciative heat. She'd been flattered by his silent attention. And dismayed to discover that even something as mundane as a family dinner could be charged with the sexual tension that sparked between them. She'd put his coffee in a to-go mug and sent him back outside as quickly as possible.

"It's not ridiculous. He's spent the last four nights sleeping in the car outside *your* house. Not mine. Not anybody else's."

"He's doing his job," Shauna insisted. "I told you about Richard Powell. Chances are, he's already skipped town. But until we find him," along with the sky-blue Buick and the identity of Yours Truly, "I've ordered a watch put on all three of us."

"Eli's an investigator, Mom, not security. He's doing this on his own time. Because he likes you." Sarah was as sure an affair between her mom and the lone-wolf detective could happen as Michael Garner and Austin and maybe even the press already suspected was going on. The rumors alone were probably already affecting her command. "Frankly, I like him. And I think you do, too."

"Don't you have papers to grade or something?"

"Not tonight." Sadie woofed and hopped to her feet. Sarah looked out the window and grinned. "Besides, the show out front is much more interesting."

Sadie barked. Twice. There had to be some sort of movement outside to get the dog's tail wagging like that. Shauna wasn't feeling that usual sense of foreboding, that sense of being watched, that had preceded all her encounters with Yours Truly thus far. But any unusual activity could be cause for alarm. She scrambled onto her sore knees to match Sarah's position at the window. "What show?"

"Seth's wrestling with that female reporter on the front lawn."

"Oh, God." Shauna leaped to her bare feet, deactivated the alarm and charged outside, with Sarah and the dog close on her heels. "Seth Cartwright!"

They were well and truly wrestling. Not talking. Not just arguing. Her over-built son had pinned that gangly Rebecca Page to the ground. The grass stain on the butt of his jeans indicated that she'd gotten in at least one good lick before he'd rolled her flat on her back and trapped her squirming legs and body beneath his. "You stay away from my family," Seth warned her. "Stay out of our business."

Eli ran up behind Shauna, hooking his Glock back into its holster. "She's been sitting outside for about fifteen minutes, using the phone in her car. I IDed her and explained this probably wasn't the safest place to be, but she chose to stay. Your son just now drove up. I guess he thought a more forcible intervention was required."

"Why didn't you tell me she was here?" Shauna demanded. She snatched at Seth's shoulder, but he shook her off, dodged a flash of teeth and spread-eagled the reporter beneath him. "Son, stop!"

"What happened to the lecture on keeping a low profile?" Eli shot right back, circling around to assist. "She wasn't breaking any laws."

"I have a right to pursue my story." Rebecca kicked at Seth's shins, uselessly trying to free herself. "My readers want to know the truth."

Seth absorbed each blow without flinching. "The second you stepped foot in this yard you were on private property. Without permission."

"Easy, buddy." Eli grabbed the back of Seth's T-shirt, wrapped an arm around his neck and pulled him off the reporter.

"Get off me!"

Eli lifted Seth to his feet and quickly shifted positions to pin his arms to control the younger, stronger man. "Not 'til you calm down."

As soon as Rebecca Page could sit up, she countered with clawing fingers aimed at Seth's face. "You jerk! I'm doing my job!"

Seth twisted against Eli's grip. "I'm protecting my family!"

Shauna pulled Rebecca to her feet and restrained her. "Both of you—stop it. Right now."

Rebecca Page struggled, but Shauna held fast. "There's never a cop around when you really need one. Now all four of you are ganging up on me?"

"I'm not a cop," Sarah volunteered, corralling Sadie by the collar. But Rebecca wasn't in the mood for humor.

"How many cops do you have watching Richard Powell?"

Shauna didn't react to the challenge in Rebecca's tone, but she found the question itself disturbing. "What do you know about Richard Powell?"

Seth jerked against the arm twisted behind his back. "Answer her."

"Cool your jets, already," Eli warned.

Fuming over his shoulder, Seth demanded, "What the hell are you doing here, anyway, Masterson?"

"That's my business, Seth. Not yours." Shauna wasn't going to be messed with. The first step to taking control of this situation was to control her son. "I don't know how they do things down at the Riverboat. But here, *I'm* in charge and *I* ask the questions."

Seth was still breathing hard, but the attitude backed off from confrontational to wary resignation. Good. One down, one to go. Shauna turned her attention to the defiant woman in her grasp. "Now—tell me what you know about Richard Powell."

"He killed two men at the Cattlemen's Bank— his alleged accomplices. Charlie Melito was a crack-head, as far as I know. He was probably involved just to get the money. But Victor Goldsmith—the banker who died—my dad investigated him." Shauna knew that Rebecca had replaced her father, a crime reporter, at the *Kansas City Journal* after his untimely death. "Dad ran out of time to prove it, but I know he suspected Goldsmith of doing some money-laundering for the same people Richard Powell worked for."

Her just-the-facts tone was laced with sarcasm. "You know, organized crime? That robbery might not have been about money at all."

Shauna had suspected that from the beginning. The papers from the vault they'd taken from Powell's briefcase had been accounting books. "So you think the robbery was just an elaborate stage for a hit on Goldsmith?"

"You're the detectives. You tell me." Rebecca turned her head to include all of them in her next accusation. "KCPD doesn't deserve its reputation. I know you've lost track of Powell. He's not in jail or the hospital anymore. Your hit man's a fugitive."

"And how did you find that out?"

"I asked the hospital staff. They know he checked out, but the jail has no record of him checking in."

"You didn't get that information from the hospital staff." Not for the first time, Shauna wondered if she had a traitor working for her. "You must have a very good friend in the department."

"I have a lot of good friends in a lot of places." Rebecca's claim sounded more like bravado than fact. "And I won't tell you any of their names."

Eli captured Shauna's attention with a single look, then inclined his head toward the porch light that had just come on across the street. "We need to move this inside or downtown."

Agreed. Time to end this conversation. "Did you have a specific question for me, Rebecca?"

"Mom—" Seth lunged forward, but Eli held him fast. "Just get rid of her. Anything she prints will cause us trouble."

"Freedom of the press is one of the rights I defend, son. Your question, Ms. Page?"

Rebecca tipped her chin up, taking advantage of the slight height advantage she had over Seth in order to look down her nose at his interference. "You were there when Goldsmith was shot, Commissioner. I want to know if you saw anything to back up my theory that it was a hit, not a robbery. After what I saw at Union Station yesterday, I thought...was that some kind of payback? Was Powell driving that car?"

Had Powell specifically lined her up in his sights at the bank? Or had Shauna simply been an unlucky target? She shivered, fearing she already knew that answer. And suddenly, unmistakably, she knew that her neighbors across the street weren't the only ones watching this party on the front lawn with interest.

She wished she could blame her bare feet on the cool grass or the night air for the chill that left her shaking. Maybe Rebecca Page would believe that excuse, but not Eli. Those eyes knew.

"Commissioner," he reminded her of his warning.

"We know that car doesn't belong to Powell, and because of the speed and the sun, I couldn't see the driver." That much she could share. But little more. Shauna released the reporter and gestured toward the street. She couldn't even tell the young woman how much danger she could be in just for standing beside her. "As to the robbery, I can't comment on that because it's still under investigation."

"I figured I'd get a stock answer."

"It's the only answer I can give you." Shauna tried to negotiate a deal for everyone's safety. "If you leave now, I promise to fill you in on all the details as soon as I'm legally and responsibly able to do so."

"That means 'goodnight,'" Seth chided.

Eli pushed him toward the front porch and Shauna linked her arm through her son's to keep him beside her. "I'll walk you to your car. Seth, take your mom and sister inside. We've already got too many eyes watching us. Ms. Page?"

She stalled at Eli's hand on her back. "I get first crack at the story?"

"You'll be the first reporter I call."

Shauna clung to Seth's arm and escorted him to the porch. She needed the warmth and reassurance that she and her children were all right as much as she wanted to get his rude butt inside and find out why he'd chosen to ignore everything she'd taught him about treating women— even pesky annoyances like Rebecca Page— with respect.

He held the door open for Sadie, Sarah and herself as Rebecca sped away in her little red sports car. "What a waste of lookin' good," he muttered.

"The leggy brunette?" Sarah asked.

Seth glared at his sister before trudging inside behind her. "The car."

Once the door was closed behind them, Seth wrapped Shauna up in a bear hug and apologized. "You know that jerk outside wasn't really me, right?"

Relieved to know his behavior was an act, not a disturbing new personality trait, she hugged him back. Shauna hated it, but understood. "A little bad press is good for your new image?"

"Yeah."

"Go hug your sister, too. And there's apple pie left over in the fridge."

With normal family harmony restoring itself in the kitchen, Shauna stepped outside to meet Eli. As he climbed up onto the porch, he asked, "Any chance of getting another cup of that delicious coffee?"

"Any chance Rebecca Page will keep her word and this incident won't show up in her column tomorrow?" Shauna hugged her arms around her middle to sustain some warmth and keep from reaching out to Eli. "Thank you."

"For what?" He joined her at the railing and they stood side by side, looking for signs of that unseen enemy in the night.

"For watching over me. For keeping my son from being arrested for assault."

"Your son doesn't like me."

"He's as protective as you are. He knows his family's in danger. He just doesn't know where the threat's coming from."

"Am I a threat?" Eli's tone was as dark as the night.

"Not the kind he's worried about."

"You've got goose bumps." So Eli had seen her shiver of awareness. "I suppose offering you my jacket is out of the question."

Shauna nodded. Enticing as it was to be wrapped up in his warmth and scent, she couldn't risk the temptation. "If it's any consolation, my daughter likes you."

"So does the dog." Eli's humor relaxed her and made her wonder if they could be just friends and colleagues once this nightmare was over. She had a feeling that if they didn't find answers soon, though, they'd bond past the point of friendship being a real option.

Too late. Despite every reasonable objection not to, she'd already moved beyond that point. She quietly slipped her hand along the railing and laced her fingers together with Eli's. It was a small gesture physically, but symbolically, it meant much, much more. She already cared deeply for this man.

She'd been lying to herself to blame stress or secrecy or danger alone for her attraction to Eli. The warmth of this simple touch soothed her, inside and out. His shielding presence beside her made her feel things she hadn't felt for a long, long time. And not even during her years with Austin had she felt a connection so intense, so right.

So wrong.

Reluctantly, Shauna pulled away and headed for the door. "I'll get that coffee now."

"Shauna." Her name alone revealed that he felt some sort of connection, too. Whether it was deep or lasting, she didn't know. But it just couldn't happen.

"Are you going back to see Donnell Gibbs tomorrow?" Work was the only topic she could allow.

"Yeah. Then I'm meeting some of the task force members."

"I'd like to come with you. Maybe the two of us working together can speed up this investigation."

"That anxious to get rid of me?"

"No, Eli. That's the problem. I'm not."

DONNELL GIBBS was counting dots again.

But between four hundred and four hundred one, his gaze darted over to Shauna, sitting at the end of the table opposite Dwight Powers. He looked again after four hundred twelve. What the hell?

Drumming his fingers on the empty envelope in front of him, Eli watched Gibbs spy on Shauna two more times while the legal eagles at the table debated the ground rules for this interrogation. Why couldn't they just get on with it?

Eli's arm ached, his mood stunk and his patience was running out. He'd been horny for Shauna throughout the whole chilly night. After Rebecca Page had gone, and Seth had followed Sarah home, the lights had gone off inside the house. While Shauna tucked herself into bed and slept in that peachy, silky second skin she called pajamas, Eli had dozed on and off behind the wheel of his Blazer. His legs were cramped, his coffee was cold and he was falling for a woman he couldn't have.

Ha! That was the ultimate irony. All those years of seeking out unattainable women just so he *wouldn't* form serious attachments, and now he was jonesing for his boss.

Last night she'd hinted that she was feeling at least some degree of the craziness that consumed him. She'd reached for his hand. They'd shared a moment. And then wham! He was left out in the cold. The woman wouldn't break the code of decorum to save her life!

He had to admire that kind of integrity. He had to respect it. But, dammit, he didn't have to like it.

This relationship that "wasn't happening" was going to end badly. It was gonna hurt like hell to walk away and return to business as usual. But what else could he expect? Wishes alone couldn't give him what he wanted. Otherwise, his parents would still be alive. His sisters would be healthy, happy campers. He'd have a partner he could trust. And he'd have Shauna.

Dwight and Audrey were debating cooperation versus self-incrimination when Donnell snuck another peek at Shauna. Enough. Eli pushed his chair back from the table and stood. "Could we just get him to look at the pictures, please?"

Audrey Kline's chin jerked up. Eli didn't need the reprimanding glance from Shauna to regret startling the younger woman. "Sorry," Eli apologized. "This isn't our only stop today. If we could have him to take a look at the photographs to see if he recognizes anyone, I'd appreciate it."

Audrey nodded and walked over to Gibbs. At the gentle touch on his arm, the black man stopped counting. "I need you to sit down, Donnell, and look at these pictures for us."

"I like pictures. But not of pretty little girls." Gibbs shook his head as Audrey led him to the table. "Those are bad. I can't have any."

Eli offered him his chair. "There are no little girls, Donnell. I just want you to tell me if you know any of these men."

Knowing Gibbs's penchant for patterns and memory, Eli spread the twenty photographs out like a concentration game. Then he stood back and let him adjust each picture into straight rows and right angles. Biting down on his impatience, Eli waited for Gibbs to pore over each photograph.

"Hey, LaTrese."

For a moment, Eli thought he hadn't heard right. But Shauna recognized the name, too. "Which man is LaTrese?" she asked.

Gibbs pointed to the mug shot of LaTrese Pittmon.

Eli pointed, too. "You know this guy?"

"We used to live together."

"Excuse me?"

Gibbs chuckled with embarrassment. "Not like that. He was my roommate. Before I went to jail."

Finding Pittmon and his Buick couldn't be this easy. "Do you remember the address?"

Gibbs recited a number off Truman Road, an address Eli knew by heart. "The Boatman Clinic? You and LaTrese were in rehab together?"

"He moved out first and I had to stay. And then I didn't have any roommate."

Jillian was in that place. With crazies and scum like Gibbs and Pittmon. Everyone there was trying to clean up their life and find a better place for him or herself out in the world. But for some, the rehab never took. Would Jillian end up in jail like Gibbs? Would some other cop be tracking her down as an attempted murder suspect like Pittmon?

Eli might be lost in guilt and second-guessing, but Shauna coolly moved on with the questioning. She picked out three photographs and set them in front of Gibbs. "Donnell, do you know any of these men?"

"You're pretty."

That snapped Eli back into the room. What the hell was Gibbs's fascination with Shauna? He liked his women below the age of eight, didn't he? Though Gibbs was proving to be a cooperative fount of possible leads, Eli wasn't thrilled with the creepy savant's interest in her.

"Thank you." If Shauna was aware of Gibbs's

unnatural curiosity, she didn't let on. She smiled and pointed to the pictures again. "Would you look and see if you recognize anyone?"

Donnell studied all three pictures as carefully as he counted dots. Finally, he pointed to one photograph. "That's Charlie."

Charlie Melito? As in dead Charlie in the gangsta clothes at the bank?

"He wasn't my roommate."

"Did you meet him at the Boatman Clinic?" Shauna asked.

Gibbs nodded and pointed to a photograph of Richard Powell. "He lived there, too. He's mean."

Shauna's green eyes snapped up at Eli. She was wondering the same thing he was.

Chilling coincidence? Or a trail they could finally follow?

Four men. One clinic to tie them together. All related to the recent threats against Shauna's life. Donnell Gibbs was the only one with the tidy alibi of a jail cell to clear him of driving the blue Buick. Charlie Melito was dead. Could either Powell or Pittmon be Yours Truly? Did one of them know the real truth about Jane Doe's murder?

Before Eli could connect the dots Gibbs had laid out, Donnell looked at Shauna again. "I've seen your picture, too."

She gathered the photos together and nodded as though having a locally famous face was no big thing. "I'm on TV and in the newspapers a lot."

Donnell squirmed in his chair. He squinted, as though trying to see Shauna in a different kind of focus. He craned his neck to see the photos in Shauna's hand, then looked at her again.

An alarm went off in Eli's head. Donnell Gibbs could remember anything he'd seen. He remembered Shauna from a photograph.

Eli squatted down beside Gibbs, who was rocking nervously back and forth in his chair now. "Where did you see Ms. Cartwright's picture, Donnell?" He took the photos and shuffled through them to find Richard Powell again. "Did this man have her picture?"

Gibbs shook his head. He turned to Eli and whispered. "It was with a picture of *her.*"

Her? Now Eli was confused. He pointed across the table. "A picture of Ms. Kline?"

"No." Gibbs was getting agitated again. "The girl with the pretty eyes and pretty dress. In the sandbox."

Dwight swore. Audrey gasped. Eli grasped Shauna's hand under the table, holding on even tighter when she tried to pull free. "You saw Shauna…" He corrected himself before she could. She'd understand his need to hold her, even secretly, if Gibbs gave the answer Eli expected. "You saw Ms. Cartwright's picture in the same place you saw a picture of Baby Jane Doe?"

Shauna's poker face remained intact. But the chill he felt on her skin was a tangible thing.

"I don't know her name." Donnell thought Eli was asking about the mutilated girl again.

"Where did you see the pictures, Donnell?"

"I don't know. It was dark. I couldn't see the numbers. LaTrese gave me a ride. It was a mean place."

"Who had the pictures?"

"I don't know." He tapped the stack of photographs. "He's not here."

"Do you remember the man's name?"

"No."

Shauna laced her fingers through Eli's and held on, just as she had last night. "Why were you looking at the pictures, Donnell?" she asked.

"So I could learn how I killed that little girl."

Chapter Ten

While Shauna met with the director of the Boatman Rehabilitation Clinic, Eli checked his gun and followed a counseling psychologist through the lobby into the heart of the complex. The therapist had recognized Eli from his intake meeting with Jillian and greeted him with a handshake.

"She's making substantial progress," he'd said. "We're not out of the woods yet by any means, but I don't think it would hurt her to have a visitor today. Would you like to see her?"

"I didn't think I could." Eli wanted to see with his own eyes that he'd done the right thing by sending her here. But he didn't want to cause any setbacks in her recovery.

Shauna was the one who nudged him forward. "Family comes before business, Eli." Not *Detective*. "I'll execute the search warrant for the files. Go see your sister. I think you need to."

"That's not why we're here."

"That's an order."

Eli obeyed.

Out front, there were Oriental rugs and leather chairs to complement the silk screens and modern art on the walls. The superficial entrance was posh and welcoming, exuding class and confidence.

But behind the lobby were padded rooms and hospital beds and locked doors, reminding Eli of the kind of space Donnell Gibbs was occupying down at the jail. There was a nurse's office. Meeting rooms, rec rooms. An indoor gym. Living spaces that looked like dormitory rooms. A backyard with a tall fence and more locks on the gate.

In every direction he looked there was some sort of supervised activity. A group session. A cooking lesson. A pickup game of basketball.

That's where he found Jillian.

"I'll tell her you're here," the therapist offered.

"No, wait." Eli stopped him just outside the door. "Is it okay if I just watch for a minute?"

"Sure. They'll be taking a break soon. You can talk to her then."

Watching Jillian run up and down the court took Eli back in time. The spiky punk cut of her hair was a far cry from the bouncy ponytail from her youth, but she still had that wicked three-point shot that could have gotten her a college scholarship. She was skinnier than she'd been, a by-product of her addiction, but she was still selfless on the court—passing to a player with an open shot instead of hogging the ball herself.

Though it was just a game of basketball, Jillian looked happy. And Eli hadn't seen happy—or sober—on her face for a long time.

For just a minute, Eli remembered how close he and Jilly had once been. She'd been pretty and sweet and innocent…and ready for anything anyone could dish out. She was just hitting her teens when their parents had died. Eli had come home from college to take care of what was left of his family. He got a job, kept a roof over their heads, and scheduled night-school classes around Jilly's basketball games so he could see her play.

Then she was off the team. Skipping school. Getting drunk and getting high. The little girl he'd loved had become a troubled teen, trying to forget she was taller than all the boys in her class, trying to forget she had no mother to learn from, no father to protect her. Trying to forget her brother and sister worked too much and set too many rules.

There were the older men Eli chased away from the house. The nights he stayed up until dawn without any sign of her coming home. Money from his wallet, gone. The college fund from Jilly's inheritance, gone. Jilly herself, gone for days at a time. Then weeks. Eventually, she'd show up at the front door, strung out, thrown out by her latest boyfriend.

And no matter what Eli did—the talks, the discipline, the counseling, calling in favors from other cops to track her down—it wasn't enough. He couldn't get mad enough, couldn't love her enough. He couldn't get her to love herself enough. He couldn't save her.

But hopefully someone here could. Hopefully, she'd turn out into a better life than the clinic's alumni he and Shauna were here to investigate.

Relief at seeing her smile couldn't erase his concerns about his decision to follow the judge's advice and place her here. Judges had sent Gibbs and Pittmon and Richard Powell to Boatman for detox and rehabilitation, too. Were those men inherently destined to return to a life of crime? Or did something—or someone—here at the clinic have a dangerous influence on them?

"Well, look what the cat dragged in." Jillian spotted him from the court as the game was breaking up. Crisp air and exercise had whipped a rosy color into her cheeks. Eli saw the beautiful girl she'd once been, and could be again.

"Hey, kiddo. It's good to see you."

"What's with the beat-up look?" She pointed to the bandage and bruises on his face. "Did some punk finally catch up with you?"

"I had an accident."

"I see." She bounced the basketball twice, then passed it to Eli. "Think fast, big bro."

He caught the ball, wondering if he'd imagined the sharpness to her voice, or if she really was just playing. He passed the ball back and she shot it into a steel barrel where the balls were stored. Nice. "I see you've still got game."

"Are you kidding? Do you have any idea how bad my knees are hurting? And I had to sit out after the first five minutes just to catch my breath." She mopped her face with a towel and straddled a bench over by the court. "Come on over and sit down. I suppose you want to know how I'm doing. Unless you're here to take me home? I can have my bags packed in two minutes. Oh, wait, I wasn't allowed to bring any of my own clothes."

Sarcasm wasn't her best color.

Eli strolled over and propped one foot on the bench, resting his elbows on his knee. He didn't want this impromptu visit to turn into another fight. "So how *are* you feeling, kiddo?"

"Well, I'm not sick at my stomach anymore, and the worst of the jitters are gone."

"How are you emotionally?"

Her laugh sounded forced. "You're one to ask. Aren't you the guy who turned his back on me and walked away without so much as a hug?"

"You don't remember? You were bawling. I held you for five minutes before the doctor said I had to go." Judging by the upturned glare, she didn't remember their goodbye—or had purposely chosen to forget. "He said a clean break would make it easier for you to transition into detox."

"Transition?" Okay. The temper was officially brewing. Both the sweet baby sister and the motivated athlete had been replaced by the cold-eyed wild child she'd become. "You know what *transition* means here, Eli? They lock you in a plain white room and strap you down to the bed. Some lady comes and babbles at you while they stick needles in your arms and you puke up your guts."

For a moment, Eli couldn't look into that accusatory face. Jillian had always loved being outdoors. She'd loved anything that involved action and movement. Being locked inside a room, unable to run or soak up the sunshine, would be torture for her. Doubly so if she was in pain or sick. "They're called the DT's, Jilly. They're not pleasant for anybody."

"I know what they're called." She jumped to her feet. "I'm not an idiot."

"I didn't say you were. But it's natural—normal—to be in pretty tough shape while the drugs are working their way out of your system." He reached out to brush aside the bangs that had fallen into her eyes. "Looks like you came out stronger for it. I'm proud of you for being here. I think you're gonna be fine."

"I'm fine now, Eli. Really. I haven't felt this good in years." She tugged at his sleeve and pleaded with him. "Why don't you just take me home today? I can stay in my old bedroom. I promise I won't be any trouble."

"I had to sell the house, Jilly. Remember? All I've got is that apartment now. With one bedroom."

"I can sleep on the sofa," she begged.

"I'm sorry, kiddo. But this is a six-week program. You're just getting started."

"Dammit, Eli!" He winced as she slapped his arm away. "I'm ready to go now! Take me somewhere—anywhere—away from this place."

Eli stood up straight, unbending. How many times had trying to do the right thing cost him her smile? "The judge only gave you two choices, and I didn't think jail was the best alternative for you."

"This *is* a jail! They still lock me in at night. They monitor everything I say or do—every time I go to the bathroom, every time I eat." She waved toward the door behind him. "Dr. Randolph's over there right now, spying on this little family reunion."

"They monitor you so—"

"—so they know I'm not sneaking in any drugs. I know, I know." Jillian raked all ten fingers through her hair. "I'm feeling better, Eli. I'm feeling good. If I'm fixed, why do I have to stay?"

"Because you're not fixed, Jilly. An addict can't be fixed. That's one of the things they'll teach you here."

"So now you think I'm some kind of loser who can't keep her act together? Thanks for the vote of confidence, bro."

Had Gibbs been in a desperate, delusional state of mind like this when he'd been brainwashed into believing he'd killed a little girl? It scared Eli to think that someone could plant an idea in Jillian's head right now—deliver this bag of coke, sell yourself to this man for some extra cash—and in her vulnerable emotional state, she'd do it.

Eli grabbed his sister by the shoulders and gave her a tiny shake, willing her to understand that his love was stronger than the demons she still had to face. And that, by walking away, he was making her stronger, too. "You may be feeling fine today, or tomorrow. But what about the day after that? Or the next? You still have to learn how to get from minute to minute when those drugs are calling. When you've got a problem to face they offer you the easy way out. You need time to regain your strength. You need to learn coping strategies that I don't know how to teach you."

"You just want someone to baby-sit me so you don't have to."

"Jilly—"

She shoved him away. "No, Eli. Just go. You've made it abundantly clear you don't want me around."

"This isn't a punishment. The clinic will—"

"Just go. We'll see if I have anything to say to you once I'm out of here."

"I love you."

Jillian snorted. "You don't know how."

She shrugged off his last attempt to make contact and marched past him to the back door of the clinic. "C'mon, Doc. I have to pee, and you don't want to miss that."

When she left, Eli turned and saw Shauna standing in the open doorway. How long she'd been there, how much she'd seen, he didn't know. She hugged her arms around her waist, a stance he'd learned meant she was cold, or she was fighting her way past some unwanted emotion.

He could relate. "Hey, Shauna."

Shauna's green eyes locked on to his and refused to let go. "It hurts when they can't see how much you love them, doesn't it?"

Eli scuffed his shoe in the dirt. Hell yeah, it hurt. He wasn't the monster here, though Jillian's parting shots sure made him feel like one. He wanted to tear something apart. He wanted to go back in time to when his world was a shiny bright place that made sense.

He wanted to walk over there and kiss Shauna senseless, then take her down in the back seat of his car or the nearest closet or wherever they could close a door, and bury himself so deep inside her that he couldn't feel the isolation anymore, couldn't feel the pain.

"Yeah." Better to start talking than to act on impulses that could only get him even more twisted inside. "Seeing Jilly was a mistake. All I did was get her riled up. I didn't help either one of us."

"If not you, then something else would have

set her off. Believe me, Eli, I understand. I was married to an addict for ten years. We can't predict how they'll react to anything, good or bad. We can't make the world right for them. They're always going to be looking for that next fix—whether it's a line of coke or the perfect deal. They have to learn how to make their own choices."

"If they can."

"That's right. If they can. And if they make the wrong ones, it's not our fault."

He rubbed at the stiff tension in his neck. "Does the regret ever go away?"

"I'll let you know."

With a sweet smile that could soothe even his growly mood, she gestured to the lidded cardboard box at her feet. "I've got copies of personnel files as well as the patient records we requested."

Right. The investigation. The antidote for guilty consciences and frustrated libidos. He picked up the box and carried it out to the SUV for her.

"Are you up for some heavy reading tonight? I'll buy the coffee if you help me find the connection between Gibbs, Pittmon, Powell and Baby Jane Doe."

"Coffee sounds good."

Holding Shauna in his arms sounded even

better. But they were in a public place and they had a job to do.

Coffee would be just fine.

THE PAIN in Eli's shoulder burned all the way up his neck to the base of his skull. Hunching over Shauna's kitchen table for two hours, sorting through the clinic files and taking notes, didn't help the aches from yesterday's run-in with the pavement at Union Station. He needed a visit to the chiropractor, a bone-deep massage—or a couple of answers to make the pieces of this puzzle fall into place so some of the tension inside him could relax.

"I've got nothing." Shauna closed the folder she'd been reading and yawned. "You?"

Nice. Aches and pains and unsolved mysteries weren't the only things keeping him tense tonight.

Shauna stretched her legs, raising them parallel to the floor. She flexed her ankles and pointed her toes in a graceful display of strength and suppleness that sent a whole new shot of adrenaline coursing through his body. Apparently, he had a thing for naked feet. He liked anything that showed off those long, gorgeous legs, but there was something unexpectedly intimate about her habit of kicking off her shoes when she was off duty around the house. Eli didn't know if it was the soft pink paint on her toenails he found so sexy, or the fact that bare toes meant at least some part of her was naked.

And Shauna naked was an idea he found very appealing.

But she had willpower enough for both of them. And while she could make him feel welcome in her kitchen for a late-night work session, he doubted she'd welcome him into her bedroom.

"Eli?"

He blinked and brought her concerned expression into focus. *Work, Masterson, work.*

"Right. Nothing here, either." He scraped his palm over the scratchy stubble on his jaw, setting aside thoughts of naked toes and warm kitchens, and pulled out the timeline he'd drawn. He set the paper on top of the scattered piles. "Other than the week that Donnell and LaTrese were roommates, there's no significant overlap to connect those four. They were separated at the clinic because they were at different stages of the program. Richard Powell was dismissed while Charlie Melito was still in detox. Charlie and Donnell shared the same counselor, but met at different times. And LaTrese was kicked out for smuggling heroin in."

"How'd he get it into a locked-down clinic?"

"Seduced a nurse's aide." He double-checked his notes. "A Daphne Hughes. Both of them did time for possession after that."

"Just when I think we're making progress, we take three steps back." Shauna got up and carried their empty mugs to the sink. "At least there's nothing to connect any of them to your sister."

"Don't worry. Your safety is still my priority." Eli pushed to his feet, clenching his jaw to mask the groan of straightening his neck and shoulders. "We'll find the clue we need to break this case, if not with this batch of evidence, then—"

"Relax. I saw you comparing names and dates." Shauna's smile was pure comfort. "I'm not the only victim here. It's okay to worry about Jillian. I know you've got a big heart inside that man-of-steel chest."

She crossed the room and patted his shoulder, urging him to sit back down. He sank back to his chair, treasuring the closeness rather than obeying the order. When her strong fingers closed over his aching shoulders, his body jolted with excitement. She kneaded the tight muscles until the tension broke and his pulse eased to a pleasant buzz of awareness.

"I'm sure your sister will be perfectly safe at the Boatman Clinic. It must be a fluke that the others were all there in rehab at one time or another."

"I like facts, not flukes."

"So do I. But Yours Truly might not be related to any of these men. There has to be something else they have in common."

Eli closed his eyes and leaned back into the heavenly massage. "None of the task force members I've talked to mentioned anything about the Boatman Clinic."

"Why would they? Once they found their man, why keep digging?" She slid her palms over his collarbone, moving to the muscles less affected by his injuries, but equally eager to receive her touch. "You think Rebecca Page is right? That Powell is working for some crime boss?"

"Gibbs isn't organized-crime material."

"But he makes the perfect patsy if you want someone to take the fall for you."

"That puts us back to square one. We have the wrong man in jail for Baby Jane's murder and a sicko on the loose who intends to punish you if we can't find the real killer on his timetable." Shauna's thumbs rubbed circles on either side of his neck. Her tender ministrations made it harder and harder to concentrate on the case, made it harder to think of her as another cop. "I wish we could come up with the right photograph to show Gibbs. Find out who it was that had your picture along with the little girl's. Whoever that is—that's our man."

"I thought about sitting him down to look through mug-shot books, but that'd be a crapshoot. For obvious reasons, I'm not that much of a gambler."

Eli hissed at the feel-good pain of Shauna's thumb pressing against a bruise beneath his collar.

Her grip instantly popped open. "I'm sorry. Did I hurt you?"

Eli snatched her wrists and pulled her hands back to his needy body. "Don't stop. You're bound to hit a bruise somewhere, but I haven't been taken care of like this since…"

Hell. He was the one who did the caretaking.

"Oh, my God. Eli." She'd folded back his collar to inspect the deep-violet-and-blue mark. The deliciously warm friction of her hands had become a frantic search. Her fingers moved down the placket of his shirt, loosening each button one by one.

"Whoa, boss lady." He tried to catch her hands. "You give a man the wrong idea when you undress him like this."

Did she have ideas? He somehow figured seduction by Shauna would be a slow and thorough process, not this urgent touch and grab.

But as she circled around him and spread the blue broadcloth apart to expose his chest, the shock on her face told him that sex wasn't what she had on her mind. *Now* he could catch her hands, and feel them cold and trembling.

"I didn't realize. Do you want an aspirin? An ice pack?" Shock gave way to the regret and compassion that deepened the lines beside her eyes and tightened the contours of her beautiful mouth.

"Shauna, I'm okay."

The dark rainbow of scrapes and bruises on his bared shoulder and torso told her a different story.

"No, you're not. I'm asking too much of you. You're hurt like this because of me."

Eli rose to his feet, intending to disprove her guilt. "Get your facts straight. I'm banged up a little because of Yours Truly. Crazy guy in the blue Buick. Remember?"

When she continued to stare with a look that was pure torture to see, Eli let her go and quickly rebuttoned his shirt. She didn't need to absorb his pain. "I appreciate your concern, but there's nothing on me that won't heal. And, when it comes down to it, I'd rather see them on me than you."

At that, she tilted her chin and looked him in the eye. "I've put you in a terrible position, haven't I? I've separated you from backup by insisting on secrecy—"

"I don't have friends who'd charge to the rescue, anyway."

"I've alienated you from the rest of KCPD—"

"We knew that going in. I.A. guys are used to not feelin' the love."

She sucked her bottom lip between her teeth, fighting the emotions ready to spill out. "I've made you a target as much as I am. I thought…" She swallowed hard and Eli wanted to reach for her. "I really thought we could find the truth."

"We will."

"But at what cost?"

Eli tried to communicate his commitment to her through that visual bond they shared. "I'm just doing my job, Shauna. I serve and protect. All the citizens of Kansas City—even the ones who outrank me."

She held his gaze a heartbeat longer, and then she did the damnedest thing and walked right up to him. She wrapped her arms around his waist and pressed her body into his, hugging him like there really was something incredible between them and she didn't care who knew it.

Rubbing her cheek against his chest, Shauna snuggled impossibly close, easing the tightness inside him, kindling a warmth that had as much to do with acknowledgment and acceptance as it did with body heat. Eli folded his arms around her and dipped his mouth to the crown of her hair. "I'm okay, sweetheart. I'm okay."

They held each other like that for a couple of endless minutes, moving closer if they moved at all. Trading comforts, sharing strength. Belonging.

But when her nipples pebbled with friction and thrust against him—when his own response to her warmth and scent and vulnerability stirred the masculine strength behind his zipper—Eli pressed a kiss to her temple and pushed some space between them.

"You want to fix another thermos of that hot coffee for me?" he asked, before he ruined the moment and took her offer of comfort and compassion to a sexual place.

"No."

He raised his eyebrows at the unexpected answer. "You're cuttin' me off?" She stood there, hugging her arms around her waist while he retrieved his jacket and tie from the back of his chair. "I can't do a very good job of guarding the place if I'm dozing behind the—"

"I want you to sleep inside tonight."

"Shauna...that could be dangerous."

She grabbed his jacket and tie and clutched

them to her as though stealing his clothes would keep him from leaving. "The security alarm is set. Mitch Taylor is sending a patrol unit around every hour to keep an eye on—"

"That's not what I meant, and you know it."

Her green eyes got *that* message, all right.

"I let the dog sleep inside. I might as well let you come in, too."

Eli laughed. "Hey, Sadie, I rate." The big Lab was zonked in the corner, snoring away. "Do I have to sleep on the dog bed?"

"You rate a little higher, even. There's a guest room upstairs. Complete with walk-in shower if you want. Maybe the hot water would help loosen up some of those sore muscles."

Eli shook his head. Getting naked in Shauna's house was a sure way to fog up his brain and miss the next time Yours Truly decided to call or pay a visit. "The doc said I needed to keep my arm as dry as possible until the new skin starts to set."

But she wouldn't be deterred. Once Shauna Cartwright had decided to break one of her rules, then, by damn, she was going to break it. "A bath, then. It's how I like to unwind. You've earned a long, hot soak." She left the kitchen with his things and headed upstairs. "I'll go draw one for you."

"I haven't taken a bath since I was a little kid."

"It's like riding a bike, Eli. You don't forget where to scrub."

"What about the neighbors, Shauna? They'll see my SUV parked outside and know I'm in here spending the night. They'll talk."

"Let them." She paused at the door to the bathroom. "Unless you'd rather sleep out in the cold, with those long legs twisted up like a pretzel inside your car?"

Good God, give a man patience. She was finally inviting him inside, finally leading him to her bedroom—where the master bath and tub were located, finally asking him to strip…and all he was going to get out of it was a hot soak for a few sore muscles.

"The guest bedroom will be fine."

Chapter Eleven

Good God, what was she thinking?

Shauna pulled back the covers and fluffed the pillows in the guest bedroom, acutely attuned to the splashes, rock-ballad serenades, and occasional curses from the naked man in her bathtub.

The problem was, she hadn't been thinking at all. She'd been *feeling*. Instead of reminding herself for the umpteenth time that Eli Masterson worked for her, she'd acted on the guilt she felt over everything she'd put him through. Her heart ached for the anguish he felt over his sister's addiction. She understood that helplessness, that sense that no matter what she did to help, she couldn't really help.

She understood Eli's pain and sacrifice.

So she could offer a friendly massage for a few aching muscles. She could give him shelter and do what she could to ease the physical pain.

She could end his isolation—and her own—by holding him, understanding him, loving him.

Eli needed somebody to care about him—to push past the sarcasm and cynicism—to ignore the reputation and see the real man. The one with the big passions and bigger heart and protective streak he wore like medals of honor across a good portion of his upper body now.

Shauna had seen the real man. She was falling in love with him.

"It would never work." She couldn't be what he needed. And it wasn't just about rules and protocol. She hadn't loved a man since Austin, and that had been a long time ago. Maybe she'd forgotten how.

She wasn't the right woman to tempt fate and break hearts and ruin careers.

A loud thunk from the bathroom startled her. "Eli?" The curse that followed warned her he was hurt. Shauna shot to her feet and ran across the hall. "Eli!"

She knocked on the bathroom door and cracked it open. She could still hear him grumbling a curse. Good. Not dead or drowned. "Eli?" The mirror had steamed over and she couldn't see his reflection. So she pushed the door wider and crept in a little farther. "Are you all right? Are you hurt?"

"You know, boss lady—first, you're taking my shirt off. Then you ask me to stay the night. Now you're walking into the room when I'm buck naked. I figured you to be the kind of woman who was more direct about what she was after."

Heat steamed through her pores at the flirtation in his voice—and she didn't think her rise in body temp had a thing to do with the warmth of the room. Shauna started to speak, but had to clear her parched throat and try again. "I heard a crash. Are you all right?"

"The only thing hurting now is my ego." With the door propped open, the fog in the room began to clear, and gradually, Eli's dark hair, his handsome, battered face and bruised broad shoulders came into view. He was grinning like a Cheshire cat. "You're peeking, Shauna."

Their eyes met in the mirror—intense and suggestive. There was an invitation issued, but she wasn't sure how to respond. "Dammit, Eli, just answer the question. Do you need my help?"

"I need you."

The humidity in the air must have filled her lungs because she suddenly found it difficult to breathe. But maybe she'd misunderstood. "For what?"

His grin turned wry and he broke eye contact

in the mirror. "Do you have any idea how hard it is to bathe with one arm hanging over the edge of the tub? It's practically impossible to wash your hair." He dropped his gaze to the soapy trail on the tile floor that led to the bottle of shampoo in the far corner. "Please?"

"Okay." After cinching up her robe to ensure everything was properly covered, she pushed the door wide open and crossed the room to retrieve the shampoo. When she turned around, she glued her eyes to Eli's curious, pleased expression. She sat on the edge of the deep, clawfoot tub, avoiding the urge to view the rest of his virile body beneath the waterline. He wanted a woman who was direct? "I'll wash your hair."

Shauna hadn't seduced a man since, what, when the twins were conceived? Somehow, Austin's recurring chatter about big trips, big scores and the big man he could be if she'd just support him a little more, hadn't been conducive to feeling frisky. But what Eli Masterson could do with a single look made the whole of Austin's amorous afterthoughts pale by comparison.

She couldn't lie about what she wanted with Eli. And he'd made it clear what he wanted from her. A relationship with him would be too complicated out in the real world. But in the privacy of her own home, in the secrecy of the night, Shauna allowed herself to ignore her head and indulge her heart.

First, she squeezed a dollop of shampoo into her palm and rubbed it warm between her hands while Eli scooted forward and dangled his forearms over either side. Then, she combed her fingers through his wet hair and caressed his scalp, taking as much care to do this job as gently and thoroughly as she'd massaged the tension from his neck and shoulders. It was like playing with wet silk. The thick locks were smooth and clingy—evocative to the touch. He closed his eyes and looked half asleep by the time she worked her way through every dark, soapy strand.

"Don't stop now." One lazy eye slit open to watch her reach over to the sink to pick up the plastic rinse cup.

"Oh, I'm just getting started. Trust me."

She dipped the cup into the water with one hand, and supported his neck with the other as he tilted his head back. She poured slowly, taking care that the water streamed across his scalp without any drips or dribbles running down his arm and soaking into the stitches or bandages there.

Shauna dipped the cup a little deeper this

time, letting her thumb just brush against his stomach beneath the water. Eli flinched. "Easy."

"Uh-huh." Once he relaxed again, she poured the water, breathing deeply herself as the mellowing scent of spearmint filled the air with each splash. "Just remember who's in charge around here."

She dipped the cup a third time, dragging the sleeve of her robe through the water. The ripples at the surface muted the startling hue of his injuries, but magnified the dimension and strength of his chest and legs. The view was both heartbreaking and awe-inspiring, and Shauna unashamedly looked her fill. She was up to her shoulder now in liquid warmth. But where the water ended, a different heat continued, seeping into her blood and flowing to every part of her body. She brushed her knuckles against his thigh and his breath hissed at her ear.

"Just what is it you think you're in charge of, boss lady?"

Shauna turned at the husky rumble to find Eli watching her intently. The twin kaleidoscopes of gold, amber and coffee-brown spoke of heat. Light. Virility. His eyes ignited a fever wherever they caressed her—her lips, her throat, her breasts.

But she wouldn't surrender control so easily.

"My tub, my rules." She boldly stroked his thigh again and there was no mistaking her ability to get a rise out of the man.

"Is my hair done?" he asked, holding her gaze just as boldly.

"*My* tub, Detective. I will tell you when you are sufficiently clean." She dumped the cup over the top of his head, laughing as he sputtered out the water streaming down his face.

As he sank beneath the water to smooth away the strands of hair dripping into his eyes, Shauna put the cup back on the sink. But before she could turn around, a strong arm torpedoed from beneath the surface and snatched her around the waist. Eli dragged her down into the tub with him. "E—!"

Shauna's squeal of protest became bubbles of laughter as he took her completely under. Just as quickly, they came back up. Water sloshed over the sides as Eli settled her squarely in his lap, her back to his chest, his right arm wedged firmly beneath her breasts. The tight confines left little to her imagination, and as the warm water soaked through her pajamas to her skin, there was *nothing* left to imagine about his muscular thighs and the bulge of interest in between that pressed against her bottom.

"I don't do rules, remember?" He tongued

the nape of her neck. "I think we'll do things my way."

He wrapped his injured arm around her shoulder and splayed his fingers at the front of her neck. With the rough pads of one finger and thumb, he tipped up her chin and turned it to the side, stretching her neck so that he could nibble behind one ear. He caught the lobe between his teeth and she shivered against the unyielding hardness of his chest. He rasped his tongue along her cheek and traced a line closer and closer to her lips, reaching the corner of her mouth. But when she tried to catch him for a kiss, his fingers tightened on her jaw and turned her lips away from his.

"Two can play your game, Shauna," he whispered against her ear. Then he repeated the same seductive process along the other side of her face—nipping and licking and teasing without ever giving her the satisfaction of that kiss she wanted so badly.

"Eli." The tub was too narrow for her hands to do more than cling to his arm or grip the sides. The tiniest of movements stirred the water so that it lapped against her breasts. And squirming for any kind of leverage only rubbed her bottom against his arousal, eliciting a moan that vibrated through his chest into hers and became her own. "This isn't fair."

"I'll tell you what isn't fair." He skimmed his fingers down her neck and dipped them beneath the collar of her robe, pushing the sodden silk across her shoulder and baring her skin to his lips. "That you..." Tiny little nips became a deeper, sensuous feasting of lips and tongue. "Can be so damn sexy." He pushed the robe and collar down her arm, exposing more of her to the cooling air. "That you respond to the slightest look..." He dribbled a palmful of warm water over the goose bumps that erupted, then soothed each one with a kiss. "Or touch..." He palmed her breast and Shauna jerked against him as hot, burning need speared her to the core. "Or kiss."

Every cell in Shauna clenched, then leaped in needy anticipation as Eli rolled her in the water and claimed her lips with his. Soft seduction and playful games were done. Water surged between them, then swept over the edge of the tub as Eli dragged her against him. She combed her fingers into his hair and clutched at his scalp. The thin layers of wet silk that separated them were no barrier to the hard warmth of his chest teasing the tingling, straining tips of her breasts. He bent one knee and wedged his thigh between hers. Shauna moaned into his mouth as he squeezed her bottom and forced her hot, aching center to ride his leg beneath the water.

"If being with you..." He kissed her chin. "...means breaking the rules..." He kissed the soft spot beneath. "...then I want to be a guilty man."

He claimed her lips again in a kiss so tender, so needy, so long and deep, that Shauna lost track of where the water from the bath ended and the moist heat that Eli stoked within her began.

But their positions were awkward, the space was cramped, and it really wasn't fair that she still had on clothes while he was gloriously naked and obviously as ready for this as she was.

"Eli..." She tried to push herself up, but shifting her weight to her knees could spoil the moment. She tried to pull herself out, but Eli's arms trapped her. *Under the water.* "Eli, stop." She dodged the mouth that tried to silence hers. "You're supposed to keep your arm dry." The next kiss skidded off her jaw. "I won't break any rule that involves doing any more damage to you."

She rose and fell on the massive sigh that lifted his chest.

"You're right." He pushed her back and pulled his feet beneath him. He grabbed a towel off the rack and tossed it onto the floor to soak up the puddles they'd made. Then he stood, rising like a water god from the deep, wet and sleek and potently male. "We can't do this."

For a split second, Shauna felt every one of those ten years that separated them. She'd borne two children, worked a tough job, survived a tougher marriage. How could she possibly please this Neptune? Of course they couldn't do this. She'd find a way to deal with the disappointment.

But as she scrambled to pull the sticky silk from between her legs so she could climb out, Eli scooped her up into his arms and she tumbled against his chest. The desire in his eyes straightened out her misconceptions even before he spoke. "We can't do this...here."

The utter determination in his voice thrilled her, reassured her, made her hungry with a need that transcended years and rules and lonely isolation. Eli Masterson wanted her. Shauna Cartwright wanted him.

They dripped on the carpet as he led her into the bedroom.

"You won't be needing these." He set her down beside the bed, peeled off her robe and skimmed her pajama top off over her head. Her pants landed with a plop at her feet. He paused a moment, literally licking his lips as her wet, naked breasts perked in the cool air. The lust in his eyes overrode any self-conscious instinct to cover herself. Her heart beat hard against the wall of her chest at the unique feminine power surging through her. Instead of hiding her attributes, Shauna reached up to tuck her damp hair behind her ears, innocently posing for his assessment. Just as she'd admired his body in the bathtub, Eli looked his fill of every dimple and curve before he groaned and turned away. "But I will need this."

He dug through his clothes folded over a chair outside the bathroom door and came back to the bed with a condom in his hand. Shauna had already pulled back the covers and climbed into the middle of the bed when he lay down beside her and gathered her into his arms.

Their slick bodies melded together in a tangle of legs and heat and bone-melting kisses. With his mouth on her breast, Eli pulled Shauna beneath him. She nearly came apart when he tested her readiness with his fingers.

He kissed her neck, her cheek, her ear, then whispered. "I want to be a part of you, Shauna. I want to be a part of something bigger than me. I want *us*."

She couldn't go there. She couldn't think beyond the perfection of this night. This moment out of time where she was a woman, nothing more, nothing less—where no outside restrictions or internalized doubts could keep her from what she wanted.

"There can't be an *us*." She framed his face in her hands and brought his mouth back for a kiss. "I'm the boss lady, remember?"

He teased her lips. "Not tonight. Tonight you're just *my* lady."

Eli completed the kiss and entered her in one erotic claim. Shauna moaned at the sweet stab of pleasure inside her. He held himself still as her body adjusted to his unfamiliar size and weight. And just when she began to relax, he pulled himself out and plunged in again. It was better the second time, and the next. And as they found their rhythm, Shauna dug her fingers into his back and gasped against his neck. "What are you…doing to me, Eli?"

"To each other, sweetheart." He propped himself up with his elbows at either side of her, his eyes piercing her as he buried himself one last time. "We do our best work…together."

Shauna cried out her pleasure right along with him as the pressure inside her exploded. Stars of light and heat and satisfaction rained down around her, leaving her exhausted but replete as Eli curled behind her and tucked the covers around them both.

Her breathing calmed and her senses returned. With a possessive hand cupping her breast and his thigh thrown over her legs, Eli soon dozed off. Shauna knew she shouldn't stay here, cocooned in the heat of his body, shielded by his tender protection—sharing in the fantasy of *us*.

But it was just for this one night, she rationalized. Come morning, she'd send Eli on his way to work before any of the neighbors or Yours Truly could spot him. She'd follow, alone, a little while later. There'd be no gossip. There'd be no threat. There'd be no relationship. Tomorrow, she'd become that lonely iron maiden of virtue again, and Eli would become that lonely outcast, the bane of cops and criminals alike. Tomorrow they'd go back to business as usual so they could get their jobs done.

Shauna covered Eli's hand with her own and snuggled closer as fatigue claimed her.

She wished tomorrow didn't have to come.

THE BARKING woke him.

Eli's eyes popped open. He assessed his surroundings by sound and touch until his sight adjusted to the dark. For a few seconds, his darting eyes were the only movement in the room. In those few seconds, he asked himself three questions.

Had making love with Shauna really been as amazing, freeing and beautiful as he remembered?

Had he truly fallen in love with the woman stirring in his arms?

And had he ever heard Sadie have such a noisy fit about anything before?

Yes.

Yes.

No.

The dog alarm. More reliable than any technology he knew.

"What the hell?" Eli threw off the covers and rolled out of bed an instant before Shauna pulled the sheet over her naked breasts and sat up.

She pushed her hair off her face. "Sadie? What's going on?"

From across the room, Eli saw the drowsy contentment of good sleep and good sex disappear as the frantic scratching and barking from downstairs registered. He could hear voices outside, too. At least two men, shouting at and shushing each other. With a bold lack of self-consciousness, Shauna scrambled out of bed and rushed to the front window.

"Dammit, Shauna. Get away from there!" He zipped up the slacks he'd tugged on and grabbed his holster and badge.

"There's a car out front. It's too dark to read the plate, but it's not the blue Buick."

She'd flipped open the slats of the shutters

to peek outside before Eli could snatch her around the waist and pull her away. Her silky skin and rounded hips were as familiar to him now as the grinding whine of a powerful engine roaring to life, and the certainty that trouble would soon follow.

Eli glanced out to check the situation himself. Two men, their upper bodies obscured by the ancient oaks lining the street, ran across the yard.

"Stay put." Pushing Shauna firmly away from the window, he tossed his holster and ran barefoot down the stairs. "Sadie, girl. Come!"

The golden Lab left her guard post at the front window and charged down the hallway to Eli. "Good girl." He left her at the bottom of the stairs to guard her mama. "Sit. Stay."

Leaving the confused, excited dog woofing and whining in his wake, Eli dashed to the door. With his gun drawn beside his head, he pulled the curtain aside and looked out to see the two men jumping into the car. Whatever they'd done, whoever they were, they were getting away.

Not this time.

He unlocked the door.

"Eli! The alarm!"

Shauna's warning from the top of the stairs came too late. Her warning couldn't stop him.

Without knowing the deactivation code, Eli opened the door and ran onto the porch.

The outside lights flashed on and off. An alarm blared to life, and, one by one, neighboring porch lights blinked on as people checked the doors and windows to see what the ruckus was about.

It was just getting started.

Squinting against the strobe effect of the security lights, Eli jumped down the porch steps and ran as car doors slammed and tires spun on the pavement. "Police!" he shouted, leveling his gun at the passenger-side window. "Get out of the car!"

But the wheels found traction and the car shot off before Eli could reach it. He fired once, taking out a rear headlight, but they were moving too fast to get a clean second shot. He chased it past the next driveway, but the damn thing was gone, just a dark speck of souped-up machinery disappearing around the corner into the night.

His feet slapped against the sidewalk and his breath railed in his chest as he slowed and changed direction back to the house. Eli scanned up and down the street for further signs of danger while he imbedded the facts he knew into his memory. Two men—one black, one white—was the limit of the description he could make. Tan sedan with no license plate. But the

Riverboat Casino parking sticker on the back window might make an APB worthwhile.

Maybe LaTrese Pittmon had gotten himself a new car. But what was the point of showing up here tonight, with Shauna tucked safely away inside, out of reach? Had Eli caught them watching the house? Had Sadie foiled a break-in? Had some note been left behind he hadn't yet found?

And then he saw it. Sadie had abandoned her post and was nosing around in the bushes that lined the base of the porch. Eli approached cautiously. At first he could only make out a shadowy bundle, like a big dog curled into a ball, asleep. Then the lights flashed on and he saw blue and white and...oh, no. The lights went off and Eli jogged toward Sadie's discovery.

"Get away, girl. Move." Tucking his Glock into the back of his waistband, Eli shooed Sadie away and knelt down to pull the still figure from beneath the bushes. The lights flashed on. "Oh, hell. Hell no."

Seth Cartwright. Dumped out like garbage. With a broken nose and enough swelling around his left eye to make Eli send up a silent prayer that the kid wasn't dead.

He felt for a pulse. Slow. Erratic. But it was there. As he pulled his fingers away he took note of the angry red welts encircling his throat. He'd seen marks like this on another man, fading with the passage of time. "Oh, God." This was no fluke, no random attack. Eli rolled Seth over to check his other injuries. "C'mon, tough guy. Wake up for me."

There wasn't even a moan.

The lights came on and stayed on. Eli reached for his cell phone, but it wasn't there. He pushed to his feet. Shauna's son needed a blanket and a doctor, fast.

He met Shauna on the porch steps. Buttoned up in a sweater over a pair of jeans, barefoot as usual, she looked young and vulnerable. But the cool-eyed expression she wore, along with the extra clothes—*his* clothes—she carried, told him the sexy temptress who'd been thoroughly loved earlier that night had been replaced by the consummate professional woman.

But even if the commissioner was back in town, she didn't need to see this. Eli clutched her shoulders and urged her back up the steps. "Call 911."

"It's okay. The dispatcher's already called and units are on the way." Her efficient clipped tones betrayed no emotion. "I got the alarm shut off, and here are your things. You'd better take off before—"

"Are you kidding me with this?" The sting of rejection cut him down to the quick. Apparently, he was the only one who'd been irrevocably changed by the closeness they'd shared upstairs.

But she laid a cool palm against his jaw and let him see a chink in her indomitable armor. "Eli, please. Later, I promise we'll—"

"Go call 911." He pushed her back up the steps. There would be no *later* for them, no *us*. Not while her son might be dying on the ground behind them. "We need an ambulance, Shauna. He's been beaten pretty badly and left unconscious."

"Who—?" Shauna went still, reading the unspoken message in his eyes. *Go back in the house. Let me handle this. I'm trying to protect you.* But his silence alone was enough to make her tremble. "Who is it, Eli?" She shrugged off his hold and scooted past before he could stop her from running down the steps. "Seth!" She threw herself down on the ground beside her son and cradled his face in loving mother's hands. "Oh, my God. Oh, my God."

Eli saw the silent sob wrack her body. He heard the whispered prayers and loving words. He wanted to go to her, hug her tightly, stand between her and the nightmare.

But Shauna didn't need the tender reassurances of the man who loved her right now. She needed a cop. And what he wanted didn't matter half so much as what she needed.

Taking careful note that there were enough neighbors spying from their windows and porches to keep anyone from getting to Shauna, Eli grabbed his gear. He was on the phone to the dispatcher while he shrugged into his shirt and jacket. He didn't waste time fastening anything, but slipped into his shoes and ran back upstairs. Once the ambulance was on its way, he had the woman transfer him to a Fourth Precinct number where he woke a sleepy Mitch Taylor.

"This better be good," the captain growled.

"Taylor." Eli identified himself and gave a quick situation report as he pulled a couple of blankets off the guest-room bed. "I don't know what you've got Cartwright working on, but the kid could use a little backup right now."

"His assignment is none of your business."

"If low-profile undercover is what you were going for, then his case is shot. His *assignment* is all over Shauna's front yard, waiting for an ambulance."

"Shauna's?"

Eli hit the stairs. "Commissioner Cartwright."

"I know who Shauna Cartwright is, Masterson." Too late, he heard the cautionary tone in

Mitch's voice. "You do know it's almost three in the morning, don't you?"

Eli swore. Of all the stupid times to carp on protocol. "Look, Taylor. The woman's son has been beaten unconscious and I'm the only one around to do anything about it right now. You can frickin' write me up if you want, but you are not going after her. You will not file one complaint or put one blemish on her record because of me. Not when she's got this to deal with. Not ever. Understood?"

"Down, Masterson. I've got nothing against the commish." Oh, but he'd be more than happy to make life hell for his favorite Internal Affairs officer? "Think about your crime scene there. It's going to be swarming with cops any minute. The press, too, with the leaks we've had around here. Maybe you'd better clear out before somebody with a looser tongue than mine shows up. I'll have someone there ASAP to debrief Seth."

Taylor hung up and Eli's anger seeped out on a heavy breath. But the resentment remained. He was odd man out. The other cops didn't need him or want him around. And Shauna had already ordered him to drop out of sight.

Behind the scenes or behind closed doors they could be a team. But in the bright light of day—or under the bright lights of her security system—the damn rules applied.

Within five minutes, it was just as Mitch Taylor had predicted. Detectives were canvassing the neighborhood. Traffic cops had blocked off the street to help the ambulance get through. Seth's tall, bald partner, Cooper Bellamy, was on the scene, searching through Seth's pockets and asking questions nobody had answers to. Where was Seth attacked? When did it happen? And why the hell is the I.A. guy here, anyway?

Couldn't any of these yahoos tramping through Shauna's front yard see that the only thing that mattered to her was that her son had been hurt? Eli hung back on the fringes of the hive of activity, watching Shauna hovering over the paramedics while they examined Seth. She hugged herself around her middle and rubbed her arms, trying to shake that chill that consumed her whenever she was nervous or afraid. Though her cool green eyes were dry as a bone now, every now and then she'd sniffle. She'd nod or give a short answer when one of the paramedics or another cop addressed her.

But she needed a shoulder to lean on, someone to care about *her,* not this efficient machine running an investigation around her. Now that they were loading Seth into the ambulance, Eli saw what that stoic face of authority was costing her. Protocol be damned. His shoulder worked just fine.

He alerted her with a look before he approached. But he didn't break stride, despite her darting looks around her. No doubt checking for an audience. "Please, Eli, I…"

He caught her icy hands between his own and rubbed some of his warmth into them. "You hanging in there?"

For a moment, she held on, but then she pulled away. "Do you know what we were doing while this was happening to him?"

"I was there. I remember."

Her eyes tilted up to his, revealing a glimpse of terrible despair. "What if we'd been on guard? Paying attention? Maybe we could have done something to help him."

"He was attacked at another location, then brought here. That tells me that someone's sending a message."

"Did you find anything from Yours Truly? There was no phone call, no note." She sniffed again. "If he wants my attention, he's got it. If he's trying to scare me, he's succeeded. If he's punishing me for arresting the wrong man, he knew exactly how to make me pay. I can't work, I can't concentrate, when my children… Seth's a grown man, but he's still my…I love him, Eli."

He fell into step beside her as they followed the gurney to the curb. "Is there anything you need me to do? Anyone you want me to call?"

"I already talked to Sarah. She'll meet us at the hospital." Shauna kept walking. But when they reached the ambulance, she stopped and braced her hand at the middle of his chest. "I asked you to help me once before. To help me find justice for a murdered little girl. Help me again, Eli. Find out who did this to my son."

"I will."

"Ma'am?" One of the paramedics called her from the back of the ambulance. "You want to ride along?"

Eli palmed the back of Shauna's neck. For a moment, he met resistance. "People will see—"

"Screw that." He bent his head and kissed her, anyway. When their lips met, she softened and leaned in to taste the strength and reassurance he offered. The kiss was deep and quick and over before too many eyebrows were raised. "I'll see you later."

Then he helped her inside, closed the back door and watched them drive away.

Though he longed to be with her, though he longed to be *allowed* to be with her, Eli let her go.

But he wasn't the only one watching her departure with longing and regret. Sadie whined at his side and stuck her cold nose into his hand. Eli shook his head and laughed. "Well, I guess no one will complain if I take care of you, right?"

After a quick chase and a game of fetch, Eli called the dog to come into the house. But when Sadie came trotting up, she had something besides the stick hanging from the corner of her mouth.

"Whatcha got there, girl?"

Eli pulled out the slobbery piece of paper and unfolded it. "Son of a bitch."

The note belonged with Seth's body. And like everything else that bastard had done, the message for Shauna was chillingly clear.

Found the real killer yet, Ms. Cartwright? How many peeple have to be hurt before you realize you've failed?

Now step aside and let me work. KCPD will be better off without you.

Be a good little girl and resine. Or that guy you're shackin' up with will find your body on the doorstep.

Yours Truly

Eli resisted the urge to crumple the evidence in his fist and ram it down the grammatically challenged bastard's throat. *That guy you're shackin' up with?* Who the hell knew he and Shauna had been together tonight? Who always had access to the commissioner so she could be reached in any emergency at any time of day or night?

One name came to mind. It didn't fit the typical profile of a man who could kill a little girl and cast her aside. But stranger things had happened.

After making sure Sadie had food and water before he locked her inside, Eli strode down to his SUV. Once he started the engine, he called Mitch Taylor back, and in a few terse sentences, told him to check the Riverboat Casino parking lot for a car sporting a shot-up taillight. Then Eli U-turned away from the clutter of police cars and drove toward KCPD headquarters.

He was about to make himself a very unpopular guy.

But if answers were the only kind of comfort he could give Shauna, one more condemnation would be a small price to pay.

Chapter Twelve

"What are you doing?"

Now that was the kind of reaction Eli liked in a woman—one who noticed him as soon as she came into the room.

So Betty Mills did have an emotional side beneath that smiling, plastic-faced facade. "Get away from my desk!" She stormed across the reception area. "Those things are personal. Private. Confidential police business!"

She scooped up the files that Eli had spread across her desk. She snatched up the loose memos and handwritten notes he'd been reading, too. He leaned back in her chair, his legs crossed at the ankles and propped up on her desk, and watched her fume at him. "I knew I didn't like you from the first moment I met you. Everything they say about you is true."

"That I'm a damn fine investigator, and I always get my man?"

Her pale cheeks blossomed with anger. "That you're as devious as your partner was, and can't be trusted. Give me that."

She reached for the appointment book that Eli held in his hand. But he held on when she tugged, knocking her off balance, and the papers tucked beneath her arms fluttered to the floor. "Now look at the mess you've made!"

As Betty stooped to separate and shuffle papers, Eli read the top line in the book. "It says here the commissioner is in her office this morning. But the door's locked and the lights are off. You wouldn't happen to know where she is, would you?"

Betty huffed a sound of disapproval. "I'm sure you know."

Eli dropped his feet to the floor. "Where is she, Betty?"

"At the hospital with her son. She called me at home and said he'd been injured and that she wouldn't be in to the office. Her son is conscious, but he can't remember exactly what happened to him beyond some kind of fight."

"I figured you'd know the details. You always know where to find her, don't you? Day or night?"

Betty stood and plopped an untidy stack of folders on the desk. "That's part of my job. But then you already knew where Ms. Cartwright is, didn't you? Just walking in the building this morning, I heard that you were with her last night. At her house. Half dressed. You're a disgrace to the uniform."

Old Betty was smart. But Eli was smarter.

"You know, Betty, I'm surprised. As long as you've been in the business, I figured you'd be a better speller than this."

"I was at the top of my secretarial class. I don't make mistakes."

"Then what are these?" Eli pulled three memos from his chest pocket, all penned on KCPD letterhead. "This is a grocery list, I'm assuming. Milk. Cheese. Macarooni with two *o*'s. Flower—f-l-o-w-e-r." He tossed it onto the desk and read the next one. "T-o-o-s-d-a-y. Tuesday's meeting postponed unto—instead of until—Friday."

"Let me see those."

"There's one more." She circled around the desk. But standing to keep them out of her reach was no problem. "Notify Task Force re BJD investigation. Internal Afaires on alert. A-f-a-i-r-e-s. You know, Betty, I've been on the job for years, and we've never spelled it like that."

Done making his point, Eli let her grab the notes so he could study her reaction. She wadded them in her hand and shook them at Eli's face. She was angry. Not worried. Not spinning the wheels inside her head to come up with a plausible excuse. "These aren't mine. I would never send out anything of this quality from this office." She was defending the pride of the office, not herself. "These are notes from Deputy Commissioner Garner. I always transcribe his rough drafts and proof his letters for him. No one's supposed to know it, but I'll tell you a secret I've kept for him if it will get you away from my desk. Deputy Garner has some sort of dyslexia. Even with a computer and spell-checking, he makes mistakes. He doesn't know it, but I proofread anything he sends out—and retype it first if there's a mistake."

Dread sank like a rock in the pit of his stomach. Betty didn't proofread *everything*. "Where's the deputy commissioner now?"

"At the press conference, I'm assuming."

"What press conference?" It wasn't on the books, but Betty still knew about it. "What's it about?"

"The commissioner's announcing a new development in the Baby Jane Doe case."

Oh, no, sweetheart. Don't go public. Not yet.

"Where's the conference?"

"She called me this morning to bring her her

spare suit from work. She'll be at St. Luke's hospital until her son gets out of surgery to repair his spleen, or something like that. I imagine they'll broadcast from there."

Damn, damn, damn. The hospital would be swarming with cops to support Shauna and Seth. But it wouldn't be enough protection. Not if *he* was there. And no one would ever suspect. Not even Shauna.

Eli pulled out his phone to call her. But she didn't pick up. How could he warn her if she wouldn't take his damn call?

"Give me the suit. I'll deliver it."

"I don't think so." Eli sat back down in her chair and tossed some papers into the air. "Fine. Fine." She waved him out of her seat and led him into Shauna's office. "I'll need the time to clean up after you've destroyed everything here, anyway."

SHAUNA TAPPED her watch. It was almost 9:00 a.m. Where was Betty with her clothes? The reporters would be gathering by now down in the lobby.

"Shauna, please. You've been up all night with Seth. You're exhausted. And quite frankly, you look it. You're about to break the biggest story of the year. Please...as a colleague, if you won't let me be your friend..." Funny, how Michael could mix criticism with contempt and still make it sound as though he was doing her a favor. "Let me handle this press conference. If they badger you for details about Donnell Gibbs's release, you might inadvertently tip your hand to this new evidence you've found."

Shauna paced the empty hospital room down the hall from Seth's. After a successful surgery, her son needed his sleep to recover. She'd known this conversation with Michael wouldn't be pretty. So she'd left Sarah to watch over her brother while Seth's partner, Cooper Bellamy, guarded the door. Austin waited in the hallway outside for a chance to visit the next time Seth was awake.

"It's not open for discussion. My decision stands. It needs to be *my* face on the front page when we do this. *My* family is the one under attack. If Yours Truly wants me, I'm going to make it easy for him. He is not going to hurt my son or daughter or anyone I care about again."

"Like Detective Masterson?"

"Give it a rest, Michael."

"He's done this to you, hasn't he? Turned you against me."

Shauna threw up her hands and walked away

from his accusatory eyes. "There was never anything between us, Michael. There was never going to be anything between us."

"I don't give a rat's ass who you screw at night, Shauna."

"Excuse me?" She whirled around, shocked to hear that much bile, even with the recent deterioration of their once-solid friendship. "This conversation is over."

When she slipped around him to leave, he pinched her arm in a painful grasp and dragged her back to the center of the room. "No. It's not."

"Let go of me." Knowing brute strength couldn't overpower him, Shauna twisted in his grip. But Michael knew all the moves, too, and if anything, his hold on her tightened hard enough to dig into muscle and bone. "Ow! Dammit, what are you doing?"

Michael jerked her against him, dipping his mouth against her ear. "What I care about, Commissioner…" He spat the word like a curse. "Is that *you* have *my* job."

Despite the heat of his body brushing against hers, Shauna shivered.

"So, unless you're going downstairs to announce your resignation, there will be no press conference for you."

"Like hell I will. This is about professional jealousy?"

"I can't be jealous of someone I despise."

He pushed her away long enough to pull out his phone and place a call. When it picked up, he uttered a single word. "Now."

Unarmed, alone and overpowered, Shauna didn't waste any time hanging around to decipher Michael's code. "Fire!" She hollered the one word she figured would get a response, no matter who heard, jammed her foot into his instep and elbowed him in the gut. Once. Twice. When his grip popped open, she ran. "Fire! Fire!"

"Shut up, you bitch!"

She reached the door, but Michael was right behind her. He grabbed her collar, then slammed her forward into the solid wood, stunning her into a moment of dizzy silence. Before she could shake off the pain radiating through her skull, he'd pulled his handcuffs off his belt and bound her wrists behind her.

Then, with his hand muffling her screams, he lifted her and threw her onto the nearest bed. When he turned away to pick up a bundle of gauze and a bottle off the tray table, Shauna rolled her legs off the opposite side. But without the use of her hands, it was impossible to stop her slide to the floor, and damned awkward to climb back to her feet. "I didn't respond to your threats when you sent them like an anonymous coward. I won't respond to this one."

"Then I'm sorry, Shauna. Dear, dear Shauna. But you're about to be unavoidably—and permanently—detained." He circled the bed and jerked her to her feet. He covered her scream with the pungent gauze, and as the room swam out of focus, she realized it was some kind of knockout drug. Something that made her hallucinate.

As her knees buckled, a black hospital orderly came into the room. *Help me.* She thought she said the words, but couldn't hear any sound.

Wait, he was the waiter from the Union Café. No, one of the hostages from the bank robbery. Oh, God, no. LaTrese Pittmon.

He caught her as she fell, picked her up as if she weighed nothing and laid her on the bed. Then they covered her up, put an oxygen mask over her face, with nothing but the toxic fumes to breathe.

"Powell's in the ambulance at the emergency entrance. You know what to do." Michael gave the order. The bed moved. Too doped up to do more than listen, Shauna cringed inside her head when he touched her face. "You wouldn't acknowledge your own shortcomings. You wouldn't scare away. Edward said he wanted someone who could heal the department when he named his successor. It should have been me. I'm the one who got Donnell Gibbs to confess. I'm the one who made that task force and all of KCPD look like heroes again."

So what? He'd recruited Gibbs through his connection to Pittmon? How did Michael know either man? And Powell was driving the ambulance? Richard Powell?

Pieces of the diverse puzzle began to fall into place. But Shauna was fading. She might be dying. And the elevator took her farther and farther away from her family, her friends, the cops who could protect her. It took her farther away from Eli—with the intense looks and passionate kisses and big, lonely heart.

I want us, he'd said.

Now, there never would be.

After Pittmon and Powell loaded her onto the ambulance, Michael climbed in for one last message. "Don't you worry your pretty little head. I'll handle the press conference for you. And I promise, in a couple of weeks, when your body's found—my eulogy for you will be very moving."

THE FESTIVITIES had started early.

Eli strode through the lobby of St. Luke's Hospital, with Dwight Powers and a special friend in a bulletproof vest following behind him. His detour to the district attorney's office and jail had cost him precious time. But it was the fastest and clearest way to give Shauna the answers she needed.

Perfect. There were dozens of reporters, and plenty of television cameras and microphones to catch the show for the six o'clock news.

Dwight pulled Donnell Gibbs up between them. "You ready to run the gauntlet?"

Eli grabbed Gibbs's other arm, intending to protect him as well as encourage him to speak the truth. He nodded. "I always did love a good fight."

Dwight grinned. "I knew there was something I liked about you."

Eli snatched Rebecca Page by the arm as they pushed past her. "Here's the scoop we promised."

At the front of the room, once the gasps and gossip and flashing lights had subsided—once Michael Garner stopped basking in the limelight and prattling on about Commissioner Cartwright's weakened state after the senseless beating of her son—Eli introduced Donnell Gibbs to the crowd and asked him one question.

"Do you see the man you told me about?"

The tiny black man could only stare at the floor and tremble for a moment. But then he looked at Eli and smiled timidly. Then he looked at the podium at the front of the room and pointed. "He's the man who told me how to say I killed that little girl."

St. Luke's finally had to be cleared so that medical personnel and patients could move freely through the lobby. Newswires were buzzing about the arrest of Deputy Commissioner Michael Garner. Impeding a police investigation, planting evidence, coercion, accessory to murder—and that was just what Eli had been able to prove in one week. Give him some time, and he'd nail the bastard for terrorizing Shauna as well.

Just like Joe—he should have seen it. The greed in his eyes, the lust for power—the attitude that the world owed him something special for doing the same job that hundreds of good, honest men and women did every day.

Once he found the right suspect, the pieces had fallen into place. Over the years, Michael had worked a number of cases. A drug arrest here. A spousal abuse case there. He'd manipulated some investigations so that lighter charges were made. And he'd often directed the lucky recipients of probation instead of prison to a stay at the Boatman Clinic. In return, they provided useful services when he needed them.

He should be celebrating this with Shauna, Eli thought. At the very least, he wanted to tell her that he'd been good as his word. He'd uncovered Yours Truly playing by his own set of rules.

As much as she loved her children, Eli didn't believe that garbage from Garner about Shauna being too overcome with grief and personal worry to be able to do her job. Something was wrong. Seriously wrong.

Cooper Bellamy tried to keep Eli out of Seth Cartwright's room, but Sarah hurried to the door and opened it. Seth turned his head on his pillow—he was pale, bruised and swollen—but the tough-guy attitude was still intact. "What the hell's he doing here?"

"Where's your mother?" Eli asked.

Sarah touched his sleeve. "Something's wrong, isn't it?"

"Did you watch the press conference?"

She shook her head. "Seth was asleep. What's going on?"

"Michael Garner's been arrested."

"What?"

There was no time to answer all the questions. "When was the last time you saw her?"

"Geez, Eli, you're scaring me."

Seth tried to push himself up on the bed. "If you've done anything to hurt her—"

"Hey—I love your mother. You better find some way to get your head around that, tough guy, because if I can find a way to make it work with her, I will."

"Wow." Sarah's sigh was just like her mother's. "You know, she likes you, too."

Like was a pretty mild word to explain the gut-wrenching fear that something had happened to Shauna that Eli wouldn't be able to protect her from or make right for her. Maybe, for the first time, he truly understood why the rules of protocol had been written in the first place. The law be damned. He couldn't put it ahead of Shauna if she was in danger. She might be strong enough to play her role and do the right thing despite her feelings, but he wasn't. He'd lost too much in life—his parents, the love and innocence of his baby sister, his partner—and his ability to trust himself, to trust that he *was* a good man who could do a little good in this world.

He wasn't going to lose her.

"Your mother?" Eli repeated, making the urgency of the situation completely clear. "If we can't account for her, then she's in danger."

"Ah, hell." Seth issued a warning that held a hint of acceptance in it as well. "You'd better be as good at tracking down the truth as Mom says you are. She left right before I dozed off—about an hour ago. Said she was going to prep her speech."

"Prep her speech? What does that mean?"

Sarah answered. "It means she's goes off to find a room by herself to practice what she wants to say."

When Eli found the room at the end of the hall with the missing bed and the blood on the door, he knew he had to find her.

And Michael Garner was going to show him the way.

Chapter Thirteen

Shauna had come to more than an hour ago, and she supposed that if she hadn't been trained as a negotiator and public spokesperson, she'd have run out of things to say about fifty-nine minutes ago. And she'd be dead.

She didn't suppose this shabby excuse for an apartment that reeked of chemicals and sweat was her final destination, either. If LaTrese and Powell had their way, they'd have shot her and dumped her out of the ambulance and been done with her. But apparently, Michael had brainwashed them very carefully. Preying on the weakness of their drug addictions, and no doubt using some of the torturous devices around the room—like the metal collar now clamped around her neck—he'd very carefully constructed a crime.

And he'd selected her as his victim.

His killers—Powell and Pittmon.

The method and place of execution were a mystery she was in no particular hurry to solve. But it must involve a phone call or some other sign that these two were waiting for.

Why had Richard Powell killed his two accomplices at the bank? Because he was "following orders." Why had Gibbs confessed to Baby Jane's murder? Because he believed the "story" Michael had taught him was real.

So what had Pittmon been trained for?

Shauna had a sickening feeling that she already knew.

"So, LaTrese—" she started. They'd moved to first names about ten minutes ago. "I understand you had a relationship with one of the nurses at the Boatman Clinic. Daphne Hughes?"

"Yeah, Daph and I had a thing." The blank look in his eyes was similar to the look she'd seen in Donnell's. He might not even remember what he'd done two years ago. "She wasn't too bright, but she was good in the sack."

"Did you get her pregnant?"

LaTrese threw up his hands and backed away. "I ain't no daddy. Those things make too much noise. They cost too much money."

But Shauna was so sure. "What was the baby's name?"

"Makayla." His chin jerked up. He knew he'd

been duped. He snatched the chain connected to Shauna's neck and dragged her off her feet. "I ain't no daddy. She ain't my little girl."

"That's because she's dead, isn't she?" Shauna coughed the words through the constriction at her throat. She was dangling, hanging. If Pittmon didn't release her, she'd be dead soon enough, anyway. But she wasn't going to die without knowing the truth. "What happened? She cry too loud? Did you shake her too much? Hit her too hard?"

"No!" The chain caught beneath her chin and dragged her higher.

Powell cursed at them from the mouse-infested futon where he'd propped up his swollen leg. "Shut up! Both of you! I can't think!" He massaged the knee Eli's bullet had shattered with the butt of his own gun. "Why doesn't he call?"

"We could just get rid of her."

"No! It's a perfect crime. We'll get away with it if we do it right."

Shauna struggled to breathe. "The perfect crime is what Michael is getting away with." She coughed, but it only dug the ring in further. "He's framed you two for murdering me. He'll walk free. You'll take the… rap." It was the last word she had air for.

Pittmon shook her like a fish on a string.

Had he killed his own daughter that way? Jane Doe? Makayla?

Eli, where are you?

The telephone rang and Pittmon dropped her to the floor. Shauna collapsed in a heap, sucking in deep breaths through the bruised muscles of her throat.

"Get it!" Pittmon crossed the room to snatch the phone from Powell's hand when the crippled man didn't do it fast enough. "It's got to be him."

"Back off. I'll answer." Powell flipped open the phone. "Yeah." He listened for a moment, his icy eyes narrowing with confusion. "But that isn't what you said before! That isn't how it's supposed to play out!" Clearly agitated by the message on the other end of the line, Powell tried to argue. "But we were only supposed to be here long enough to switch out vehicles. Where the hell is Pittmon's car?"

Shauna laughed to get their attention. "This isn't the first plan that hasn't gone right, is it, Powell? You weren't supposed to get shot at that robbery, were you? You hadn't counted on Eli Master—"

"Shut her up!"

Shauna scrambled like a crab to escape Pittmon's charging fist. The first glancing blow knocked her to the floor. The second blow never came.

"Police! Open up!"

A battering ram smashed through the door and both men reached for their guns.

Eli crashed through before the S.W.A.T. team. He dove to the floor and rolled. "Drop it!"

The exchange of fire was brief. Eli took out Richard Powell before he even got off a shot. Shauna kicked out, knocking Pittmon off his feet. His shot went wide and the big man went down, wounded, before the special team swarmed in and secured his weapon and his fists.

"Shauna?" Eli hurried across the filthy room and unhooked the collar from her neck. "Bastards." He smoothed gentle fingers around the welts on her neck. "Are you hurt?"

"I'm okay." Those dark gold eyes conveyed so much—relief, anger, fear...love. "Nothing serious." She twisted around to show him her bound hands. "A little help?"

Amidst another bout of swearing, he retrieved bolt cutters from a team member and cut the chain between the cuffs. They'd figure out the rest later—for now it was enough to ease her shoulders back into their normal position and have Eli massage her chafed wrists. "You *are* hurt. Dammit. I didn't figure it out in time."

"But you did figure it out?" Smart guy.

"Yeah." At last she saw the crook of a familiar smile. "I've got Yours Truly handcuffed in a police car outside. I brought the whole cavalry. He's not going anywhere."

Neither was Richard Powell. And LaTrese Pittmon, she hoped, would make Dwight Powers's year. "I know who killed our Jane Doe. Makayla, I mean. Makayla Hughes. I can finally put her name on that grave marker. I think a DNA test will prove Pittmon's not just her biological father, but her killer. I don't know if he figured out how to dispose of the body on his own, or if—"

"—Garner told him how. There are a lot of messed-up people in this case, Shauna."

Shauna smiled. One thing, at least, was perfectly clear. She tried to reach up and stroke his handsome, battered face, but her fingers were still numb. "I want to touch you."

"Me, too. Shall we get out of here?"

Her knees were still weak from whatever knockout drug Michael had given her. But when she stumbled, Eli swung her up into his arms and carried her outside. "I've got you, boss lady."

"Eli, your arm—"

"Can hold you just fine." He carried her outside to a circle of police cars. Mitch Taylor was there. Cooper Bellamy. Michael was in the back seat of one of the cruisers. So that's why he'd been so late making the call to Pittmon and Powell. And Eli stood in the center of it all— part of the circle, an outcast no longer.

"I've got you." He kissed her then. Kissed her in front of a dozen KCPD detectives and uniformed officers. He held her tightly, taking his sweet, leisurely time to break the rules.

When he finally raised his head, Shauna was flushed and needy and scared at how much she loved this man.

"I've got you. And I don't care who knows it."

"No. I REFUSE to accept this." Shauna looked at the badge and gun and letter of resignation on her desk. Then she looked up at the tall, wonderful man who'd walked into her office this morning, intent on throwing his career away.

"I need you more than I need this job."

She reached into the drawer of her desk and pulled out her own letter of resignation. "I typed this up last night. After we…made love."

"Which time? In the shower or in the kitchen?"

"Eli!"

The glow of mischief never left his eyes as he circled her desk and took her hands, letting his thumbs gently stroke her healing wrists. "This city needs you. KCPD needs you. They need a leader with a conscience—someone who enforces the rules—with heart."

"But, Eli—"

"No buts, boss lady. You can't quit."

"You're not the boss of me."

"You're not the boss of me anymore, either." He snatched her resignation and tore it in half before she could reach it. "Stay. On the job." He sat on the edge of the desk, V'd his legs and pulled her between them. "And with me. Dwight Powers offered me a job as an investigator at the D.A.'s office. It might actually be nice to go to work someplace where people are glad to see me."

"Are you sure? I'm ten years older."

"I'm ten years smarter. Smart enough to fall in love with you."

Shauna reached up and touched the scar at his temple, the one he'd earned the first day he'd entered her life. "Seriously, Eli. I love you for it, but don't do this for me."

"I'm not. I'm doing it for *us*."

Then he gathered her in his arms and kissed her like the equals they were. She kissed him back. Yeah. Shauna liked the sound of that. *Us* sounded perfect.

* * * * *

RUN, ALLY! Don't be fooled by him. He's evil. Don't let him touch you!

But as the forbidding figure came through the mists toward her, Ally knew she couldn't run. His features burned with dark malevolence, and his physical domination of everything around him seemed to hold her like a net.

She'd heard the tales. She knew all about the Wolverton legend and the ghost that haunted The Willows, an elegant old mansion lost by Micha Wolverton nearly a hundred years ago. According to folklore, the estate was stolen from the Wolvertons, and Micha was killed, trying to reclaim it. His dying vow was to be reunited with the spirit of his beloved wife, who'd taken her life for reasons no one would speak of, except in whispers. But Ally had never put much stock in the fantasy. She didn't believe in ghosts.

Until now—

She still didn't understand what was happening. The figure had materialized out of the mist that lay thick on the damp cemetery soil. A cool breeze and silvery moonlight had played against the ancient stone of the crypts surrounding her, until they joined the mist, causing his body to thicken and solidify right before her eyes. That was when she realized she'd seen this man before. Or thought she had, at least.

His face was familiar…so familiar, yet she couldn't put it together. Not with him looming so near. She stepped back as he approached.

"Don't be afraid," he said. His voice wasn't what she expected. It didn't sound as if it were coming from beyond the grave. It was deep and sensual. Commanding.

"Who are you?" she managed.

"You should know. You summoned me."

"No, I didn't." She had no idea what he was talking about. Two minutes ago, she'd been crouching behind a moss-covered crypt, spying on the mansion that had once been The Willows, but was now Club Casablanca. And then this—

If he was Micha, he might be angry that she was trespassing on his property. "I'll go," she said. "I won't come back. I promise."

"You're not going anywhere."

Words snagged in her throat. "Wh-why not? What do you want?"

"If I wanted something, Ally, I'd take it. This is about need."

His words resonated as he moved within inches of her. She tried to back away, but her feet were useless. "And you need something from me?"

"Good guess." His tone burned with irony. "I need lips, soft and surrendered, a body limp with desire."

"My lips, my bod—?"

"Only yours."

"Why? Why me?" This couldn't be Micha. He didn't want any woman but Rose. He'd died trying to get back to her.

"Because you want that, too," he said.

Wanted what? A ghost of her own? She'd always found the legend impossibly romantic, but how could he have known that? How could he know anything about her? Besides, she'd sworn off inappropriate men, and what could be more inappropriate than a ghost? She shook her head again, still not willing to admit the truth. But her heart wouldn't play along. It clattered inside her chest. The mere thought of his kiss, his touch, terrified her. This wildness, it was fear, wasn't it?

When his fingertips touched her cheek, she

flinched, expecting his flesh to be cold, lifeless. It was anything but that. His skin was smooth and hot, gentle, yet demanding. And while his dark brown eyes were filled with mystery and wonder, there was a sensitivity about them that threatened to disarm her if she looked too deeply.

"These lips are mine," he said, as if stating a universal fact that she was helpless to avoid. In truth, it was just that. She couldn't stop him.

And she didn't want to.

* * * * *

Find out how the story unfolds in...
DECADENT
by
New York Times *bestselling author*
Suzanne Forster.
On sale November 2006.

Harlequin Blaze— Your ultimate destination
for red-hot reads.
With six titles every month, you'll never guess
what you'll discover under the covers...

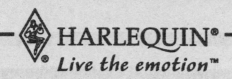
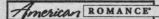

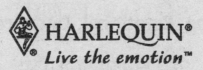

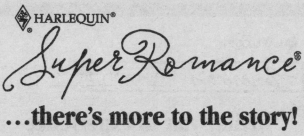

...there's more to the story!

Superromance.
A *big* satisfying read about unforgettable characters. Each month we offer *six* very different stories that range from family drama to adventure and mystery, from highly emotional stories to romantic comedies—and much more! Stories about people you'll believe in and care about. Stories too compelling to put down....

Our authors are among today's *best* romance writers. You'll find familiar names and talented newcomers. Many of them are award winners— and you'll see why!

If you want the biggest and best in romance fiction, you'll get it from Superromance!

Exciting, Emotional, Unexpected...

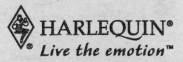

HARLEQUIN®
Live the emotion™

HARLEQUIN®
Presents

The world's bestselling romance series...
The series that brings you your favorite authors,
month after month:

Helen Bianchin...Emma Darcy
Lynne Graham...Penny Jordan
Miranda Lee...Sandra Marton
Anne Mather...Carole Mortimer
Susan Napier...Michelle Reid

and many more uniquely talented authors!

Wealthy, powerful, gorgeous men...
Women who have feelings just like your own...
The stories you love, set in exotic, glamorous locations...

HARLEQUIN®
Presents

Seduction and Passion Guaranteed!

HPDIR104

Harlequin® Historical
Historical Romantic Adventure!

*Imagine a time of chivalrous
knights and unconventional ladies,
roguish rakes and impetuous
heiresses, rugged cowboys
and spirited frontierswomen—
these rich and vivid tales will
capture your imagination!*

*Harlequin Historical . . .
they're too good to miss!*

SILHOUETTE *Romance*®

Escape to a place where a kiss is still a kiss...

Feel the breathless connection...

*Fall in love as though it were
the very first time...*

Experience the power of love!

Come to where favorite authors—such as

Diana Palmer, Judy Christenberry, Marie Ferrarella

and many more—deliver modern fairy tale
romances and genuine emotion,
time after time after time....

*Silhouette Romance—
from today to forever.*

Silhouette®

Live the possibilities

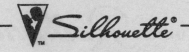

SPECIAL EDITION™

Emotional, compelling stories that capture the intensity of living, loving and creating a family in today's world.

Desire

Modern, passionate reads that are powerful and provocative.

Romantic SUSPENSE

Romances that are sparked by danger and fueled by passion.

SILHOUETTE Romance

From today to forever, these love stories offer today's woman fairytale romance.

BOMBSHELL™

Action-filled romances with strong, sexy, savvy women who save the day.